HYPER OBJECT

Volume 2

Written By

Shae Moloney

Created By

Kyle Keller & Mark Sidener

outer
giant

HYPER OBJECT

Volume 2

Written By

Shay Moloney

Art by

Kayla Keller & Mark Sidener

Hyper Object Volume 2

Published by Outer Giant LLC
St. Paul, Minnesota 55104
outergiant.com

Story originally published at hyperobject.ink

Written by Shae Moloney
Book Cover and Illustrations by Matt Owen
Original story and characters by Kyle Keller and Mark Sidener

1st edition 2026
Printed in the United States of America

ISBN: 978-1-970738-01-8

Contents

CHAPTER 10
Lees the Seer

Lees had never wished for a lamp or light box more in her life. What little light came from the few Rapidite-dust torches that lined the narrow passage barely illuminated the path ahead. Her boot splashed into yet another puddle she hadn't seen, soaking the last dry part of her pants. Lees fought the rising urge to yell out in frustration.

It had been like this from the moment Jez pushed her through the hidden door at the end of the alley. The two limped down the dark, twisting tunnels that pitched downward at an uncomfortable angle. Lees' shoulder ached from keeping her arm slung around Jez's back to help her balance on her good leg. Every time Lees slowed to ask one of the thousand questions swirling around her mind, Jez waved impatiently and urged her to keep moving.

They'd been walking for what felt like hours. The tunnel was silent save for the sounds they made – rhythmic thumping of their three feet, the occasional grunt of pain, and now the wet slap of fabric against Lees' leg with every other step she took.

"So, secret tunnels under the town, huh?" Lees tried.

"Mhmm," Jez hummed. With her next one-footed hop, her foot caught on the uneven ground and rolled to the side. She winced and paused, panting.

"They're under the whole town. Old service tunnels. They run under pretty much everything and go far, far beyond Last Light," Jez continued.

"Service tunnels for what?"

"When they were first built? Probably carrying supplies to the mines. But now, well," Jez gave Lees a knowing look. "We use them for other stuff."

"What stuff? Like... like *drugs*?" Lees asked. Jez rolled her eyes to the ceiling and shook her head.

"No, not that. C'mon, hun, you know what I mean. The stuff you can't get this far down. Things you can only get in the Quarters. Or the Oppri," Jez added. When Lees continued to look mystified, Jez flicked her fingers against the collar of Lees' new coat. "Like this little number. How do you think something like this made it all the way down here?"

Jez signaled for Lees to put her arm back so they could continue.

"I didn't grow up here, how would I know!?" Lees said

indignantly. They reached a fork in the tunnel, and Jez pulled Lees to the right.

This new tunnel – still unnecessarily dark and wet, in Lees' opinion – ended abruptly at a wooden door, which opened to reveal a short set of stairs leading to a narrow room with an identical door at the far end. Though the room must have been carved out of the surrounding rock, the walls and floor had none of the telltale unevenness or drill lines Lees expected to see. No machine she knew of could have made such perfect angles.

The whole room was bathed in a yellow-blue hue thanks to a blown-glass vase filled with Rapidite chips near the door. As Lees' eyes adjusted to the dim lighting, she noticed a short bar top had been cut directly into the stone. Three mismatched wooden chairs sat against the wall opposite the bar, resting on a well-worn knotted rug. It felt almost homey, but surely Jez didn't live here...?

"Ach!" Lees shouted. Two of Jez's bartenders, Eylii and Midge, popped up from behind the bar moments after Lees and Jez limped into the room. Eylii, the youngest of Jez's crew, wore a guilty expression and kept her hands pointedly hidden behind the bar. Midge's eyes widened at the sight of the injured pair. She hurried toward them with a half-full bottle of kudri sloshing in her hand.

"Jez! Are you okay? What happened?" She asked. Lees carefully deposited Jez into one of the wooden chairs and backed away to let Midge get closer.

"D'you get the doctor?" Jez asked. She swatted Midge's hand away before she could touch the wound on her leg.

"Bausch is on it. He'll be returning any minute now," Midge replied. She pulled her hair back with a handkerchief as her eyes scrutinized Jez's leg, then turned to visually catalog Lees' many injuries.

"Good, good. Now get me–" Eylii cut Jez off by thrusting a drink into her hand. Jez laughed and patted the younger woman's arm before accepting it. "Thanks, E."

"I know what you need, boss," Eylii said. Lees watched with narrowed eyes as the bartender brushed a strand of blond hair from her shoulder, still grinning at Jez. She blinked in surprise as Eylii turned those bright blue eyes on her, asking, "You want anything, Lees?"

"Got anything with bubbles?"

Midge forced Lees into a chair and gently dabbed her open wounds with a washcloth to clean away the blood and grime. Lees tried waving Midge away as Jez had, but Midge smacked her hand away as if she were an unruly child. Lees huffed.

"Bubbles, bubbles, bubbles... hmm, nothing like that down here. How about, uh," Eylii squinted at the bottle Midge had been holding. "Some good ol' fashioned dusty brown stuff?" She jiggled the bottle cheerfully.

"Sure," Lees said with what she hoped sounded like enthusiasm. Midge wasn't fussing over her anymore, but it wasn't because the woman was respecting her wishes to be left alone. Midge was staring at her, head tilted to the side, as if she were a puzzle to solve. Jez was too busy draining her amber-colored drink to notice.

"What?" Lees whispered.

"I just can't believe it. It really was you calling out in the bar," Midge said.

"MIDGE!" Jez and Eylii roared in unison.

Lees looked between the three of them in confusion, but nobody elaborated.

"What's she talking about?" Lees demanded. Jez gently set the empty glass on the ground and pulled herself upright. The movements looked painful, but nobody dared offer her help.

"Well, you sort of appeared to us –" She began.

"To Jez!" Midge interjected, too excited to contain herself. Lees knew the woman loved a good bit of drama, especially when the late-night shift came into the bar bustling with petty gossip.

"Yes, to me," Jez said. Midge literally shrank back at the look Jez shot her. "Earlier at the Eye of Mite, your face appeared behind the bar in a cloud of dust. Scared the hell out of a couple regulars."

"What are you talking about?"

"It was seriously spooky," Eylii piped up. She refilled Jez's glass and lifted it to her hand. She offered a refill to Lees', but hers was untouched. "You spoke, too, but your voice was all wrong. It was like, mechanical – or no, that's not the word, like... like stone. Like a whole bunch of stones grinding together."

"You broke so many good bottles, I can't even imagine how much it cost –" Midge said. Jez flicked some of the kudri in her glass at her to shut her up.

"Sorry, I have no idea what you're talking about," Lees said, but then something horrible rolled over her – a moment in the fog of the fight suddenly resurfaced.

All three women leaned in at the sudden look on her face. "Oh, no. The vision. I was fighting Meshi, that new kid, and I guess I asked for help. Then it showed me – well, I saw a vision of you, Jez. I thought I was imagining it. What...what did I say?"

Midge pressed her lips together as if to keep from smiling. Eylii held her own glass and the bottle up to her chin and fluttered her eyes, imitating what must have been a version of Lees' mechanical voice to say, "Oh Jez, you're so amazing, you're perfect, *GRAAAH-pshew, crrrashhh,*" Eylii mimed glass shattering around them before pouring four clear-colored shots. She paused, shrugged, and said, "And that was that."

Bile crawled up the back of Lees' throat as heat flooded her face. She leaned forward to grab and drain her glass. The burning, oily liquid carved its way down her throat to her stomach. She kept her eyes focused on the glass.

"Okay, you've had your fun, knock it off," Jez snapped.

Midge and Eylii locked eyes and fell into a fresh fit of

laughter. They clinked their shots together and downed them simultaneously.

Lees slumped to sit on the ground with her back against the wall, wishing there was a hole she could crawl into instead. The pleasant warmth of the alcohol spread from her stomach to her extremities, soothing her aching muscles. Exhaustion descended on her all at once, and Lees found herself struggling to keep her eyes open. Each blink heavier than the last, until the quiet darkness behind her eyelids overtook her.

BAM! One of the doors in the hidden room swung open with a bang, and Lees jumped, smacking her forehead against the chair she'd been leaning on. Sleep clung to the edges of her eyes, and to her horror, she'd drooled on herself. *How long was I out?*

Lees wiped her mouth and pulled herself up, nearly doubling over in pain from her stiff joints and partially healed cuts on her hand.

"You didn't tell me how heavy this guy is!" Bausch griped. The Eye of Mite's security guard-slash-bar back muscled his way through the door with Ike in tow.

Dr. Hayes walked in behind them casually, as if heading into a routine exam. Gripes prowled in after him with a bulging satchel clenched in her jaws.

"Place him on the bar, I suppose," Dr. Hayes said. He rolled up his sleeves, then set his bag down next to Gripes' satchel. Without another word, Bausch saluted Jez and stalked back out the door, pulling it behind him as he left.

"Ike, I can't believe you're alive!" Lees shouted. She staggered over to him, wincing at the pain shooting down her arm.

"And what happened to you?" Dr. Hayes asked. He raised an eyebrow and pointed at Lees' bruised face and bloody arm.

"Nothing, I'm fine," Lees said quickly.

"So am I," Ike grumbled.

Lees tried to back away from Dr. Hayes when he turned her arm to inspect the damage, but something stopped her. Half a dozen strands of yellow Hyper extending from beneath his coat pressed gently against her back to hold her in place. She hadn't even noticed he was shaping.

"You are very much not fine," Dr. Hayes said flatly. The yellow Hyper strands branched out further, some ushering Lees to sit on the bar next to Ike while others pulled back Lees' collar and shirt sleeve to expose her injuries.

Lees felt like a child on the exam table being poked and prodded. Ike sat stoically next to her, his head bowed and shoulders sagging. Lees tried to sit still.

With his patients no longer resisting treatment, Dr. Hayes stretched out both arms to begin his work. All shapers looked like orchestra conductors to some degree, but the doctor's shaping was more like watching a gory performance. With one hand, he orchestrated the yellow Hyper strands to clean Lees' wounds, while the other addressed Ike's injuries. Each strand danced in unison with the doctor's movements. He used his own hands to inject anesthetic, then directed strands to carefully stitch torn tissue back together.

Dr. Hayes continued his one-man healing show in relative silence, muttering to Gripes every so often as he stitched, applied compresses to bruises, and checked his patients' vital signs.

"This ain't so bad. I've been hurt worse," Ike assured them around a thermometer. In his elevated position on the bar with his shirt unbuttoned, everyone in the room could clearly see scars and burns covering the man's body.

"Perhaps," Dr. Hayes said good-naturedly. He used a needle-thin piece of Hyper to stitch a two-pronged cut on Ike's arm, calmly continuing his work while explaining, "But you sustained multiple lacerations across your arms and chest that could lead to substantial blood loss if not addressed. Not to mention you reopened the wound I tended to earlier today."

Lees watched Ike's expressionless face as the doctor tugged the wound back together. Not even so much as a wince.

"Sorry to cause you so much trouble, doc," Ike said. "Promise you won't have to do it a third time."

Two strands of yellow Hyper wrapped a piece of cloth doused with something pungent around the blossoming bruise on her side. Lees wrinkled her nose at the smell, which was something between rotting fruit and old meat. A third strand tightly cinched the binding to hold it in place. Despite herself, she gasped when their light touch sent shockwaves across her body.

"Your bruising looks worse than it is, but this bandage should stop the swelling and reduce your pain. The trick is a concoction of fermented triiock juice," Dr. Hayes told her. A strand of Hyper offered her a bright red, cherry-flavored lollipop. Lees smiled and stuck it in her mouth.

He turned back to Ike and asked in a tone that was more curious than accusatory, "Now. Please elaborate on why you didn't fight back against the boy. Size certainly wasn't an issue."

"You didn't fight back?!" Lees shouted incredulously. The lollipop dropped from her mouth, and a tiny yellow strand plucked it right back in.

"It's complicated," Ike grunted. He was pointedly avoiding eye contact with her. Lees tried instead to focus on the sweetness coating her tongue from the candy to quell the angry heat brewing in her stomach. She could see Meshi's sneering face, could feel his joyous rage as he delivered blow after blow.

Lees placed a hand on Gripes' head. The purt stayed diligently by her side, purring loudly.

"Why did you bring him here?" Lees finally asked. She flexed her jaw to crunch down on the lollipop and grind the candy into a fine powder. Her tongue dug into the grooves of each tooth to dislodge the sugar crystals. Nobody seemed to know what to say, so she did this in complete silence before continuing. "You brought that asshole into our town. He dragged me down into the mine, dug up this stupid rock, and tried to kill me. And then you. For what?"

"You still have it? The Hyper Object?" Ike asked quickly. He looked stunned.

"Seriously? That's all you care about? You can have it," Lees hopped down from the bar and used her gloved hand to pull the object from her hip pouch. Jez let out her breath in a hiss when it appeared, its many points sparkling in the Rapidite light. Lees held it out, then chucked it at Ike's chest. Dr. Hayes leapt out of the way, and Midge pulled Eylii back.

Ike picked it up and held it in his bare palm. Jez gasped, and the doctor slid in front of Gripes to shield her from whatever happened next.

But nothing happened. Ike tossed the stone in the air and caught it, then repeated the movement.

"Might as well be an ordinary rock. To us, at least," Ike slid off the bar. From this angle, Lees could see there were three or four fresh two-pronged stab wounds on his bicep and forearms.

"In my professional opinion, you should sit back down," Dr. Hayes said, but didn't move to intervene. He unwrapped a blue lollipop for himself and leaned against the wall. Gripes spun in a tight circle before plopping down at his feet.

"What did he do to you?" Concern overtook anger as Lees got closer to Ike. He had another set of stab wounds, fresh and weeping, in the meaty part between his shoulder and neck. She reached toward him, but Ike pulled his collar tight to hide the cuts.

"He failed to be the person I thought he was," Ike said. He held out the Hyper Object pinched between his thumb and forefinger. "But that doesn't matter anymore. Now we need *you* to be the person you're supposed to be."

"What's that supposed to mean?" Lees snorted.

"There's something special about you. This stone will only speak to you, and that means you're the only one who can wield it," Ike held it out for her to take, but Lees backed away.

"Talking to that thing doesn't make me special. It makes me dangerous. You don't know anything about me, you just want access to that thing," Lees snapped. Ike maintained eye contact, unfazed by her reaction or the pointed stares from everyone else in the room.

"Take it."

She tried to look away, really she did. But Lees felt the pull, and finally glared down at the tiny stone in his hand. Dried blood still clung to its points from when it tried to consume her. The room shifted out of focus. Her vision narrowed on the red sphere. A voice in the back of her head pleaded with her, reasoning with her, begging her.

This wasn't safe. It wasn't safe.

Don't do it.

Don't do it.

Do it.

Do it. Don't. Do it don't do it doitdoitdoit

She reached out for it in her mind, mentally covering the space between her brain and the stone. In an instant, chaos and violence erupted around her in the form of overlapping visions. Mine explosions. Trains derailing. Blades, pipes, glass. Screams of overlapping fear and agony that left her ears ringing and blood pressure rising.

It reached a fever pitch, and Lees swayed on the spot.

Ike crushed his fist around the stone, breaking the connection.

Lees wheezed and collapsed against the bar. Jez lunged out of her chair and caught her before she fell to the ground.

"What are you doing to her?" She spat at Ike.

"Proving my theory. Look at how it calls to her. She's a Seer, I'm sure of it now," Ike said.

"Seer?" Eylii asked.

"It's a shaper who can talk to Hyper," Midge whispered back.

"Talk? No, no. That's like saying shapers bend Hyper. Seers commune with Hyper. They share thoughts and visions, hopes and dreams, form bonds, even – well, you get the picture," Ike explained reverently. He looked around the room but landed back on Lees. "*This* is what Meshi wanted, but he didn't make the cut."

"Ironic, the person he duped into leading him into the mines is the one who ended up being its Seer, huh?" Jez said.

Ike nodded. "No doubt in my mind, kid. With this stone, you're now the most powerful Seer in the world."

CHAPTER 11

Answer the Call

There was a strange energy in the secret bunker. Midge and Eylii stared slack-jawed at Lees. Jez glared at Ike with a look that could melt steel beams. Ike looked at Lees in wonder, as if she were a mortal turned god. Dr. Hayes – well, he seemed pretty unaffected by the whole thing.

Ike continued on despite the stunned silence.

"My question is, how'd you get past the Oppri? They've cataloged every Seer there's ever been, and there's no way they'd let one down this far. I mean, they're closely monitored," Ike mused. "It's a big deal."

"Then you know the *weight* of this accusation," Jez snapped. She leaned into Ike and held out her hand. Ike tipped the Hyper Object into her palm, and she quickly pocketed it. "And make no mistake, that's all this is. An accusation. A guess."

"Excuse me, are you also injured?" Dr. Hayes interjected. Hyper darted out from under his coat, pulled a chair closer to him, and guided Jez into it so he could examine her leg. "Goodness. What could have caused this?"

"Me," Lees said softly. Dr. Hayes lifted an eyebrow but said nothing. Lees sighed. "With Hyper. I didn't mean to."

"So you *can* shape Hyper?"

"I didn't mean to," Lees repeated. "But I wasn't going to not fight back." This comment was aimed at Ike before she looked back at the doctor. "I knocked Meshi out with a pillar of Hyper, too."

"You got a whole pillar from that teeny little stone?" Eylii asked incredulously.

The doctor nodded thoughtfully. "From what I saw, the stone appears to be sufficiently dense enough to accomplish that. You can see it in its dark red hue."

Dr. Hayes continued this line of thinking, and Lees could hear him and Jez talking, but it was as if the volume in the room was suddenly turned down. Her mind raced at the accusation Ike was leveling at her.

Mites can't be Seers. Grandmother spent years trying to prove I could be trained, but I failed. I could never shape her Hyper, could never respond to it or call out to it. It never spoke to me. This can't be true.

But then why can I feel what the Hyper Object is feeling?

"Lees? Hey, Lees, listen to me," Jez was saying. Lees snapped her attention back. "Lees, this guy's full of it. You don't have to do anything you don't want to."

"How do you know what wielding Hyper feels like?" Lees asked.

"Huh?" Jez said.

"Back in the alley, you said 'the first time hits hard.' How would you know that?"

"Oh, you know, it's a common saying. It's... oh, hell," Jez sighed. "Because I've shaped Hyper before."

"I knew you had a connection!" Ike interjected.

"Oh, you did not. And shut up, you're not part of this," Jez growled.

"You're a shaper? When did you find that out? Why have you been hiding it? And why do you live here in Last Light?" Lees blurted out question after question. She couldn't help herself.

Was Jez some undercover shaper assigned to a secret mission down here? Is Jez a runaway teen who discovered shaping while on the road?

No, that would be crazy. She's just a beautiful, talented shaper who... lied to you.

"Slow down, hun. I'll answer your questions, whatever you wanna know. Just calm down," Jez replied. "You really scared me, you know. Hyper can be super dangerous."

"I know. I'm sorry, it's just the only shapers I know have been doing it their whole lives. Or they're dicks about it. I've always wanted to be one. Knowing you're one, but you don't use it for personal gain, it's... refreshing? It's nice," Lees finished lamely.

Jez motioned for Lees to come closer. She placed her hand behind Lees' neck and looked at her. Lees felt her cheeks flush and was acutely aware of the other people in the room.

"I don't know if you're a Seer or not. But I need you to understand that shapers don't see what you saw. They can't commune with Hyper or command it like you do. Whatever you are is beyond a regular shaper," Jez sighed and touched her forehead to Lees', who turned a brighter shade of red. "That stone is horrifyingly powerful."

Jez pulled back to look Lees in the eyes, then tilted her head to whisper in Lees' ear, "You're your own person. If you decide to be this, I'll teach you what I know. Just... be careful."

Lees swallowed hard. "I will."

The two parted, and Lees waited for her heart to slow to a normal rate.

"I'm starting to understand this connection with the stone, or at least that it seems to *want* me," Lees spoke slowly. Blurry visions tugged at her from the back of her mind, tantalizingly just out of reach. She tried to ignore the sensation, to control the intruder's thoughts in her head.

"But I don't want it."

Grinding machinery shrieked in her head. Flashes of

dancing oranges and yellows darted at the edges of her vision. The noises, smells, and images grew in intensity the more she tried to ignore them.

"It's like it feeds on the darkest parts of me. These visions beg me to hurt people who might hurt me, to kill people in my way. If all this thing can do is obsess over suffering, then I wish I'd never found it!" Lees spoke louder and louder to combat the high-pitched whining that filled her ears.

The room fell silent as she screamed. Eylii slowly hooked a finger into an empty glass and pulled it toward her. Midge slid the bottle over.

Ike spoke up first. "What you want doesn't matter anymore. The object chose you. It's up to you whether you accept it or let yourself be consumed by it. You might not think it's fair, and maybe it's not, but the Hyper Object has a reason for choosing you."

"That's bullshit," Jez snorted, which turned into a strangled yelp as the doctor performed a rather painful step in the process of stitching her leg up. Lees gripped Jez's hand.

Ike looked at Jez, then the others in the room. His face was a mess of emotions, but Lees could clearly see the strongest one showing through – regret.

"You might not understand what's at stake yet, but that's all right. You will. You're right that I helped make this mess. I got you hurt, and all of you involved. This wasn't how we intended for it to go down," He admitted.

"Oh, this wasn't the plan?" Jez mocked. She put weight

on her injured leg to test it, then gave Dr. Hayes a thumbs up before putting herself between Lees and Ike. "What exactly did you think would happen? You brought a lunatic into our city to go on a little scavenger hunt for a mythical item, and you thought everything would work out nicely?"

Jez jabbed a finger in his chest, and Ike flinched.

"Nobody was supposed to get hurt. Nobody was even supposed to know what we were doing."

"Since you're on the other side of this, I'm gonna let you in on a little secret, *cutlass*. When your lot shows up, someone always gets hurt," Jez leaned in closer and snarled, "Unfortunately for you, this time that *someone* is under my protection. If anything happens to her from here on out, I'll personally hunt you down and gut you where you stand."

Jez and Ike faced each other with murderous intent written across their faces. Neither so much as blinked. Liquor filled and overflowed the glass Eylii was filling as she watched the scene with an open mouth. Dr. Hayes had another lollipop in his mouth and watched the scene with his arms folded over his chest.

Nausea sank into Lees' stomach like a cold weight, an unwelcome companion to the frustration welling in her chest.

"Would you two back off?" She shouted. It was hard to say whether Jez or Ike looked more shocked.

"Ike, you're not wrong," Lees began. "You did create this nightmare for all of us, but you also stood up for me against the little psycho." Ike's expression softened, a small smile pulling at the corner of his mouth. "So you can't be *all that* bad."

"And Jez. I know you're going to protect me, and that's part of what I love—" Lees stopped herself and tried to pivot mid-sentence, "Looove to see. With my friends. However, Meshi is still out there somewhere, so we need to work together to find him."

"I still don't think this is your fight," Jez said.

Ike nodded quickly and turned for the door.

"Hey, where do you think you're going?" Lees said. Her commanding tone stopped Ike in his tracks.

"To find Meshi?"

"Neither of you is listening to me. I know I said I don't want the stone, but I have it, and it's my responsibility to deal with it. Good or bad, I need to learn how to use it, because I think I'll need it," Lees said.

Someone knocked on the door a moment before it crashed open. A chipper Lees didn't recognize leaned into the room, gasping for breath while struggling to say, "Jez! Jez – *oh gods* – a train's just arrived."

"Midday?"

"Yeah, midday. There's a cutlass knight on it," His eyes widened, and Lees realized he wasn't winded; he was struggling to speak out of fear. "They grabbed Teeg."

Lees' blood ran cold, and all hope for a peaceful talk with Meshi and whoever sent them vanished.

"Woodrow and a big group of miners are at the station confronting them," The chipper continued.

"That little shit…" Jez stole a glance at Ike, who had the decency to look down to avoid her gaze. She turned back to Lees. "This changes things."

Lees held up a hand to stop her. There was no point trying to convince her now. *They grabbed Teeg.*

"Listen, you gotta know the risks. I don't know if I can pull you out again. You were half mad when I found you last time, and if you use it again…" Jez argued.

Lees held out her gloved hand and wiggled her fingers. "I'll only touch it through these, and I won't use it unless I absolutely have to."

Jez's shoulders eased a fraction of an inch. She reached into her pocket to hand over the stone, but stopped when her fingers touched it. The stone vibrated wildly in her closed fist the closer it got to Lees. Jez furrowed her eyebrows and searched Lees' face, then nodded and handed it over. Lees wondered what was going through Jez's mind, but this didn't seem the moment to ask.

"All right, people!" Jez shouted, suddenly all business. Her employees and the chipper stood to attention. Here was that commanding presence Lees was used to. "Eylii, Midge, if our girl is going out there, we need eyes on the situation. Head topside and figure out what's happening. Tell Bausch to get down here and stay by the doc. We're gonna need him if things break bad."

"We need to move," Ike warned. He bounced on the soles of his feet.

Lees wrapped her arms around Jez and squeezed. When the women separated, Lees kept her arms locked tight around Jez's forearms and took her in for a moment longer. Her stomach fluttered, either from Jez's smile or the stupid plan, she couldn't say. Before she could lose her nerve, Lees darted in to press her lips to Jez's.

Midge howled, and Eylii nearly fell over behind the bar. Lees pulled away, caught one look at the smirk on Jez's face, then practically sprinted out the door with Ike in tow.

Don't overthink it, don't overthink it, you have to focus, Lees chanted in her head, willing it to be true. She could analyze the moment a hundred times over once Teeg was safe back home.

Ike quickly caught up to Lees and led them through the tunnels back toward the manufacturing district. Her pants were soaked once again by the time they spilled out into the alleyway. Ike rolled his shoulders and wrists to loosen his stiff muscles. He seemed a bit lighter on his feet now.

"Meshi won't stop, will he?" She asked bluntly.

Her question was met with a lingering silence.

"No," Ike said finally, struggling to organize his thoughts. "He's willing to hurt anyone to get that stone. Whatever knight he's with will gladly help him for a little extra pocket change."

"Then we'll stop him before anyone else gets involved. And you're going to help me."

Ike nodded in confirmation, signaling he'd do what he could to fix the mess he helped create, only to realize she wasn't talking to him.

Lees' eyes fixed on the pouch swinging back and forth on her hip with every step. Her hand instinctively moved to caress the object's tiny spikes still covered in her blood. It might have just been the adrenaline or her imagination, but through the layers of the pouch and her glove, the stone oozed a deep, pulsing heat.

CHAPTER 12

The Bloodsoaked Enforcer

Windows and doors shuttered and bolted shut across Last Light as Lees and Ike raced through the alleyways toward the town's central thoroughfare. The streets were eerily empty. Those who didn't want to cross paths with the cutlass, or who knew better than to challenge their authority, appeared to be hunkering down to avoid any unwanted attention. Lees couldn't blame them.

She'd heard countless horror stories about the way the Oppri's soldiers dealt with so-called problems. The handful she'd encountered herself back in the Quarters were the same. They were mean-spirited brutes who threw their weight around, using the maximum amount of force possible, always acting before asking questions. Their neighbors missed a midsummer tithing once – Lees never found out why – and a pair of cutlass dragged Mr. Torks into the street before beating him in front of his family. Lees' mother closed the curtains tight, but it didn't drown out the sound of their laughter when Mrs. Torks threw the money at their feet and begged them to stop.

Lees shook her head to clear away the memory. She had to focus. Ike's injuries kept him a few paces behind her as they ran, so he had to leap forward to grab her arm before they reached the end of the alley. A couple of boys who couldn't have been older than 15 raced past. One of them held a dented water pipe that had no doubt been pried off an unfortunate window unit somewhere.

"You gotta be smart if you're going to try to fight this knight," Ike warned. Lees nodded and tried to turn away, but Ike held her arm tight. She searched his face and found nothing reassuring in his expression. Ike continued in a low voice, "Even the lowest-ranked knights are cutlass-trained. They won't hesitate to kill you, so be ready for the worst. Let's see your stance."

Lees stared at him, frozen. Ike widened his stance with slightly bent knees, then waited for Lees to imitate him. Somewhere down the street, the din of voices was rising. The braver or stupider folks of Last Light were gathering. She should be there. She needed to be there, but instead she sighed and squatted down.

"Keep your center of gravity low, don't lock your knees," Ike corrected. He raised his fists in front of his face, keeping his elbows tucked in a boxer's stance. He nodded pointedly until Lees did the same. "Don't open yourself up to any hits you can avoid."

Ike swung his fists slowly, landing mock blows against Lees' shoulder, side, head. She tried to protect herself, but every time she moved her fists, he targeted a different area. She couldn't keep up. Lees could feel the pressure rising in her chest, her face hot as she suffered fake blows in this childish mock fight. Ike swatted her hands to knock them away, then dropped his own and backed away.

"Have you, uh, ever actually fought anyone?" Ike scratched his head and began to pace as he spoke. Blood rushed to Lees' face, and her ears stung with the sudden heat. The murmuring of angry voices beyond them suddenly rose in pitch.

"No, I mean, not exactly, but..." She floundered. Ike looked her over and continued pacing, and the weight in her chest deepened. All the bravado she had storming out of the underground bar vanished in an instant. "It doesn't matter, though, I have the Hyper Object. It'll protect me. It protected me against Meshi. I beat him!"

"And it almost killed you, remember?" Ike said. Lees' heart sank. Was he losing faith in her? Had it all been an act in front of Jez, him thinking she was special? "Look, most of these cutlass knights are going to be bigger than you.

Stronger, even. But being small has its advantages. You'll be faster than them, so keep that in mind."

He held up his hands again, and Lees resisted the urge to smack him and run away. She bit her lip to stop from shouting – *this isn't helping! Are you already giving up on me?* Something fluttered in the corner of her eye, the beginnings of a vision or some other omen from the Hyper Object, maybe. Lees squeezed her eyes shut, took a deep breath, and swallowed frustration smoldering in her stomach like hot coal.

"We don't have time for this. I need to get to Teeg. We'll figure it out when we get there."

Lees backed up one step, two, then darted out of the alley into the street before Ike could stop her. He smacked one fist into the palm of the other hand in frustration and shouted after her, but she was already gone.

The crowd was even bigger than it sounded. Seemed to Lees like half the mining crews had come out to confront the cutlass knights. It was no wonder. Most of the people living here had some reason to despise the omnipresent pressure from the crown in the form of these power-thirsty authorities.

This can't end well, Lees thought. She pressed herself between people and shimmied side to side to reach the front. Most people she recognized, especially the old timers who had been in Last Light since its infancy. Some carried their drills and hand axes, while others clutched bottles or shovels. Everyone had something in their hands. From this vantage point, Lees couldn't see much of what was in front of them, but Teeg must be up there somewhere.

She continued worming her way through the crowd, trying to jostle as few people as possible.

"Careful, kid," Someone muttered. Lees turned to see Hove, a miner on Teeg's standard crew. The woman bumped the person next to them with her elbow to make room. Lees hurried through the gap, keeping her eyes down to make sure she didn't step on anyone's toes, until something stopped her in her tracks.

"Leave this area immediately, and you will suffer no harm!"

Meshi. She couldn't see him from where she stood, but the voice was unmistakable. That weasel must be close, probably standing up on the train platform so he could look down on the town. The burning coal in her stomach flared, and before her eyes she saw Meshi's face stretched to hideous proportions and baring monstrous fangs. She placed her hand gently over the pouch, as if to calm the Hyper Object, to silently say, *now is not the time.*

The pompous threat did nothing to calm or disperse the crowd. People were growing more agitated by the second, shouting and pressing in on her from all around. Lees focused on keeping her footing as the crowd's movement carried her forward. She squeezed between her agitated neighbors until she was finally deposited at the bottom of the stairs leading up to the train station platform.

One of the men from the alley – Woodrow, Lees thought – was struggling against two other people in the crowd who were holding him back. These men, she didn't recognize.

Lees looked up frantically, searching for the man who let her into his home, fed and looked after her, who embraced her like family. Where was Teeg? But then her eyes fell on another familiar face.

Just there, under the station's awning, stood Meshi. He paced defiantly at the top of the stairs, hands planted on his hips as he scowled at the crowd, clearly upset his threat hadn't landed. The upper crest kid looked better than she could have imagined after the fight they'd had. Except for the dried blood staining the collar of his white shirt and a swollen lip, nobody would have guessed he'd been unconscious in a puddle of his own blood just a few hours ago.

How is that even possible? Lees wondered. Meshi hadn't seen her yet, and confronting him before knowing where Teeg was felt like a bad idea. Lees darted back into the safety of the crowd and peered over the flannel-clad shoulder of the daytime mine chief. She couldn't stand the sight of Meshi's smug face any longer. Her eyes raked over the scene until she finally saw him.

Lees winced at the sight. Two cutlass squires clad in obnoxious golden helmets and leather armor that glittered with woven strands of gold held Teeg's arms behind his back. Their efforts to keep him still were pointless, as Teeg's head hung down limply, and he wasn't moving. His face was barely visible beneath his shaggy, greying hair, but the parts Lees could see were bruised and raw. His lip was split, and a cut across the bridge of his nose dripped blood steadily onto the ground. Lees' hand tightened over the pouch as if on instinct. The object buzzed angrily.

Another man was on the platform, sitting just to the left of the scene. He wore an enormous gilded suit of armor that put the other cutlass squires' uniforms to shame. Lees couldn't tear her eyes away from it. Each of his broad shoulders was adorned with the roaring head of a lion expertly crafted from iron and gold. Intricately carved plates overlapped beneath the lion's fangs like hardened fishscales to protect the armor-wearer's upper arms, leading down to the spiked balls covering the elbows. Tiny, uniformly curved lines covered the glittering chestplate, winding downward toward a linked latticework of diamond plating at the torso.

He was perched comfortably on one of the platform benches with his helmet resting next to him. An empty pint glass and an open carton of chewed rib bones sat beside the helmet.

The armored man seemed unbothered by the whole scene. He dabbed his face delicately with a napkin before stuffing it inside the carton, then opened his mouth to pry a bit of rib meat from between his teeth.

"Mmm, tricky son of a bitch. Think I got it. Gotta hand it to 'em, they know how to cook a mean rib."

He didn't say this particularly loudly, but Lees caught

every word above the noise of the crowd. She watched, stunned, as he turned to face the crowd and smiled, as if seeing them gathered there was a happy surprise. The man ran a hand through his wavy blond hair and tucked a loose curl that had fallen over his forehead back in place.

"Well, hey there, folks," He finally said. "Forgive my rudeness. I haven't introduced myself yet. I'm the Cutlass Knight Enforcer."

The shouting died down almost immediately. Lees' ears rang from the sudden silence. She stood on her tiptoes to get a better look. The Enforcer had an impossibly wide, square jaw with uneven stubble, as if he'd been too busy to shave today. He didn't move from where he sat and watched the crowd with a bemused look for a few seconds.

"I'm told there's a young woman here who has something she shouldn't. My team's looking to bring her in for questioning, but for the life of us, we can't seem to find her anywhere," He said. His voice had a slight drawl to it that Lees recognized from somewhere but couldn't quite place. Surely she'd remember coming across someone like this before, right?

Lees stayed half hidden behind the daytime mine chief and took another few steps backward. Someone put their hand on her shoulder, and she flinched, but it was just Hove again. The woman patted Lees a few times reassuringly and shook her head.

"I assume you've all gathered to help us look for her? A little townwide search party?" The Enforcer asked. The shock of the Enforcer's presence had worn off a bit, and the crowd was building back its courage. A few people towards the back of the crowd booed and shouted their disapproval.

"No? I suppose that must mean she's not here," The Enforcer made a big production of shrugging his enormous, lion-clad shoulders toward the other squires gathered at the base of the platform.

"That's a lie!" Meshi darted forward and turned to address the crowd. "I know she's here. You worms are hiding her somewhere in this filthy town. Just hand over Lees if you don't want to meet the same fate as this big idiot." He jerked his finger toward the crumpled form of Teeg.

Not wanting to provoke an armoured knight was one thing, but there wasn't one person in Last Light who was going to let the likes of Meshi insult or order them around. People around Lees started shouting obscenities and moving around again. Someone threw a trash bag toward the platform, and the plastic snagged on one of the squire's daggers and split open, spilling its contents everywhere. A few rocks sailed over her head, but none of them hit any of their intended targets – *probably for the best,* she thought.

Everyone seemed rightfully distracted. Lees edged her way behind the front row of the crowd, then scrambled forward to close the distance to the platform.

Teeg noticed her first. He locked eyes with Lees just as she stepped away from the crowd. Without hesitation, Teeg swung his arms around to his front, dragging the two squires holding him forward with the force. He pulled himself out of their grip effortlessly and stood up, teetering slightly before finding his balance – *what did they do to you?* Lees thought desperately – then made his way up the last few steps to stand before Meshi and the Enforcer. He towered over them, placing himself between them and Lees.

The Enforcer remained seated, but cocked his head and grinned.

"Impressive," He said, miming applause. "But all that bravado isn't going to accomplish anything. How's this? I'm willing to make you a deal and look the other way at your 'manhandling' of my guards. Just tell me, where is this Leeee-zuh hiding?"

Teeg glowered. Lees could practically see the waves of anger rolling off the normally even-tempered man. But she could also see the very real bruises and cuts marring his body, and the way his jaw clenched with each breath.

"Nobody by that name lives here," Teeg said. Then, after a pause, spat, "And it's *Lees*."

Encouragements and agreements erupted behind them as the crowd shouted their support. Meshi began to yell again, directing his anger at the crowd once more, but the Enforcer waved to silence him.

The Enforcer slowly stood up with a groan and flexed his shoulders. He picked up his trash, turned to Meshi, and held out the box and pint glass for him to take. Lees snorted at the sight of the kid rushing to grab the garbage and shove it into a nearby receptacle.

"Hey, you better recycle!" Someone shouted. Meshi scrunched up his face, but said nothing.

Now that he stood face-to-face with Teeg, Lees could see that he was even taller than Teeg. The Enforcer was a behemoth in his oversized suit of armor. She'd strain her neck looking up at him if she were standing as close as Teeg was now.

"I don't usually repeat myself, but you've had your bell rung pretty good, so I'll make an exception. Are you ready to be reasonable this time?" The Enforcer asked softly.

Teeg didn't back down. He hadn't moved an inch since getting up to the platform. He took a long look at the man's armor and face before shrugging and saying, "Depends."

Lees barely had time to register the smile that crept across the Enforcer's face before his fist connected with Teeg's gut with such force that the crowd could hear the ribs snap. He buckled and fell to his knees.

For a moment, the town stood still. Teeg gasped on the ground with the Enforcer watching, Lees froze, and the entire platform fell silent.

And then the crowd collapsed inward. Lees was shoved from behind and slammed into the shoulder of a person who had darted in front of her. All senses were lost in the chaos. Voices shouting with anger and crying out in pain erupted from every side. A few unlucky souls fell and were trampled in the stampede heading toward the Enforcer and Meshi. Those with weapons had them raised, those without were readying fists, all in a mad rush to tear these interlopers limb from limb.

Lees focused solely on keeping her feet planted on the ground. If she fell, she'd be useless. She needed to get away from the crowd. There's no way she could use the stone this close to people without someone getting hurt.

An explosive boom followed by a wave of concussive air and dust sent the crowd reeling in all directions. Those far ahead of Lees grabbed their heads, and she could see dribbles of blood trickling out of their ears. Her own ears were ringing painfully. A wide-shouldered man in front of Lees tripped backward, taking her and a few others with him to the ground. She wheezed as the air was knocked from her lungs at the impact.

What the hell was that? She focused on wriggling out from under the man and regaining her footing.

"Do you really think you stand a chance against me!?" The Enforcer shouted. His voice pierced through the fog of dust still settling. Lees watched in horror as it settled to reveal the Enforcer kneeling inside of what could only be described as a crater in the platform. His fist was still connected with the ground where he'd punched it down. Brilliant spikes of yellow Hyper surrounded him, as though they'd erupted from somewhere below the street, blasting the concrete stairs apart and ripping through the railings.

"When Meshi said this was a town filled with drunks and idiots, I should have believed him."

When the Enforcer stood up, the Hyper retracted with him. Hyper spikes melted, joined together, and weaved up his body. Lees could see now the utility of the armor: small holes decorated the chest plate and arm plating, leading to the reservoir below that housed the plasma-like Hyper. The majority of it wound its way up his arm and into his right shoulder, where it pulsed in excitement. The lion's hollow eyes danced with it now, and the effect was mesmerising.

"I am a knight of the Holy Cutlass Order," He said. He flexed his arms, and the Hyper glowed even brighter. Lees' heart jackhammered in time with its rhythm. "I am the roar of the Exalted One. I am the Bloodsoaked Enforcer."

Tiny spikes of Hyper poked out from the holes across his armor. The Enforcer turned to fully address the crowd now to deliver the final message, "I am your superior in every possible way. You will obey me."

Lees realized too late that the people in front of her had skittered away from the danger, leaving her standing out in the open.

Meshi's voice grated on her ears as he began shrieking, "There she is! That's her! I knew she'd come crawling back for that dirty old miner!"

The Enforcer cocked his head to the side. The Hyper around his arm flared to life with the movement, sending little tendrils dancing along the channels in his armor down to his wrist once more.

Those in the crowd who remained had backed up against the buildings lining the central thoroughfare. Most were scrambling through alleyways to escape the area, having lost their nerve against this Hyper-wielding beast. Some were injured enough to need help limping away, and Lees vaguely hoped Dr. Hayes was still on call down in the hidden bar room.

"*This* is the girl? That little one there?" The Enforcer asked through a laugh. He shook his head at Meshi. "You're telling me you were bested by this frail thing? She's a child!" Then he turned fully to Meshi to look him up and down. After the assessment, he reached out an enormous armor-clad hand to pat the top of his head. "Hah! I guess I can see how. Well, don't let it get you down. Those upper crusties just don't make Hyper wielders like they used to."

Maybe in different circumstances, Lees would enjoy watching Meshi be humiliated. But not now. Lees clenched her fists so hard her nails dug grooves into her palms. Through the ringing in her ears, she could hear her own heartbeat racing wildly. Every *thump* forced white-hot anger through her veins.

Images of the Enforcer's armor cracking in the grip of an enormous crystal hand flooded her vision. His face growing redder and puffier until it popped like a bug. She saw yellow Hyper no longer under his control slithering up the lion armor's chestplate to constrict around his neck and squeeze tighter, and tighter.

This time, Lees didn't tell the Hyper Object to stop. She didn't fight against it. She *liked* what she was seeing.

"Small doesn't mean weak," Teeg wheezed. He pushed himself off the ground and stumbled over to stand between the Enforcer and Lees again. "An important man like you would do good to learn that."

The Enforcer scoffed. Teeg didn't break eye contact with the Enforcer, even as Lees stepped to his side and placed a hand on his back.

"You should run," He said. "Best not to go toe-to-toe with this guy."

"Not a chance. I'm not running, Teeg. Not this time," Lees said.

"Is that the boy from the cave?" Teeg gestured to Meshi, who looked utterly unamused.

"Sure is," Lees responded.

"Kind of ungrateful, ain't he?"

Meshi began to roll his eyes, but stopped as Ike finally appeared. He was winded and looked angry, but stepped right up next to Lees. Teeg shot a questioning look at Lees, who waved her hands in a noncommittal way. There'll be time to explain later.

Ike said nothing, but Meshi began to cackle both at his former bodyguard's wounds and his decision.

"You can keep him. The dumb dog seems to have taken a

liking to you, and I have no use for disloyalty," Meshi sneered as he said this to Lees.

"Damn. That kid sure is a prick, huh?" Teeg grumbled. He looked down and grabbed Lees' arm in surprise, turning it over in his hands as if looking for something. Only the tiny cuts remained as evidence she'd once been nearly consumed by the bright red Hyper. "You know how to use that rock now?"

Lees turned in surprise. "How did you know?"

"Jez isn't the only one in this town who keeps track of things," He said.

She smiled back and nodded. "It's a work in progress, but Ike's got me covered."

Hearing this, Ike shuffled a bit and nodded.

"*Ahem,*" The Enforcer said. He snapped his fingers, and the two armored squires appeared at the top of the stairs. Between them, they carried a large lion's head made of iron. It must have been at least two feet wide. They stepped forward and dropped it with a thud next to the Enforcer.

"As touching as this little moment is, I'm growing bored. I really don't care about any of this," The Enforcer whined.

"Then leave," Lees snapped. She peeled off her gloves and took up the stance Ike had taught her back in the alley – one hand raised to protect her face, the other over the pouch on her hip. She thrust her chin to the left. "Train's right there."

A few more people had crept back into the square to join those standing near the buildings. Lees could hear them again, not quite back in fight mode, but definitely not backing away. The lack of further stone-crushing explosions helped.

It's like a switch flipped. The Enforcer's face dropped, and his eyes narrowed. His Hyper sparked and pulsed as he pushed energy into it, an effort Lees could feel even from where she stood.

"Hand over that stone, or I'll tear this whole place to the ground," He threatened through gritted teeth.

Her heartbeat reached a fever pitch as adrenaline coursed through her. Lees' vision sharpened as the fuzziness remaining from the concussive explosion faded away. She tried not to think about the pain from the Hyper piercing her skin or the darkness of its void; those would be problems for later, when the fight was over. She needed to do this, and it needed to be now.

Lees unsnapped the top of her pouch and let the deep red light of the Hyper Object shine out.

The glow elicited varying levels of shock in the crowds across the street, which quickly turned to speculative excitement. Everybody in Last Light liked a good fight, after all.

A wicked smile flitted across the Enforcer's face. He snapped his fingers once more, and the two squires darted into the city in opposite directions. A few tried to slow one of them down, but the squire made quick work of knocking them to the ground.

Some people branched off to follow the squires, but even more stumbled back when the Enforcer sauntered toward the trio with heavy, determined steps. His attention was solely focused on the young, defiant woman in his path.

Faster than she could have reacted, the yellow Hyper on his arm flared to life and exploded out of him. She flinched, but it wasn't aimed at her or Teeg. The strands converged into a single beam that shot into the mouth of the iron lion. Its eyes and open mouth glowed with the swirling Hyper as the entire contraption lifted off the ground with ease.

Ike tapped Lees on the shoulder. "Showtime. Just stay focused, and don't let the visions overcome you."

"Thought you said you figured it out!?" Teeg asked. Lees ignored him, instead pushing him gently behind her so she could focus on the Enforcer. Or should she watch the lion head?

Ike continued, "He's likely a power hitter, so remember what I said. Use speed to your advantage."

"What does that even mean?" Teeg asked in a panic.

"Teeg, I love you, but you need to chill," Lees replied.

The lion's head looked almost weightless under the control of the Hyper. It was carried up and positioned just over the Enforcer's right shoulder.

Lees and the Enforcer locked eyes. She tried her best to keep her face devoid of emotion, to hide her fear. Her fingers danced just above the pouch. The light from the Hyper Object splashed across her face, bathing her in red. The Enforcer hesitated. *Was he reconsidering his approach? Was he intimidated by the Hyper Object's power in her?*

These were foolish thoughts. The Enforcer slammed his foot down and let out a bellowing, ground-shaking scream. His eyes now blazed with raw fury, unfiltered and unleashed toward the only thing he sought to destroy – her.

CHAPTER 13

Clash of the Shapers

The Enforcer's roar was still echoing around the square when a concussive explosion boomed from somewhere near Last Light's west side. Rumbling aftershocks hit them all at once, followed by an ominous column of smoke rising from the second tier near the food district.

Lces tore her eyes away from the Enforcer, breaking eye contact for only a second to survey the scene, but it was long enough. Taking advantage of the chaos, this beast of a man thrust his arm high into the air to manipulate the Hyper that was holding the lion's head aloft. Bright yellow strands drained from its orifices until they solidified into a twisted jagged handle. Enough Hyper remained inside to make its eyes dance menacingly. The Enforcer wrapped one hand, then the other, around the colossal Hyper-infused weapon and smirked.

Reverberations of several more small explosions rumbled so intensely it rattled her teeth.

"Run!" Lees shouted. She shoved both men at her sides just as her assailant brought the hammer down with incredible speed. Ike and Teeg both managed to leap out of the way, but they were not the true targets of the screaming lion.

Almost without thinking, Lees' left hand skated down her hip and into the pouch to grasp the Hyper Object, now almost hot to the touch. The multifaceted object burrowed itself into her palm, and Lees winced as she thrust her own fist upward to meet the hammer. Tiny pinpricks of pain radiated from where her skin touched the Hyper, and the muscles and ligaments along her forearm and shoulder burned with the effort.

Stay focused, stay focused, stay focused, Lees chanted silently.

Against her better judgment, Lees squeezed her eyes shut and summoned the memory of the stone pillar she'd used against Meshi, only this time imagining it bigger, stronger, exploding out from her arm with every ounce of strength she could muster. Fragmented images flickered above, below, and within the mental image until it abruptly cleared, and her vision went red.

The Hyper Object responded. Crystalized Hyper, blood red and glistening, erupted from the sides of her fist and the space between her fingers. Lees braced herself for the agonizing pain, but it was distant this time, as if happening somewhere beyond her. The squirming plasma-like substance of the Hyper itched uncomfortably where it spread across the back of her hand, crawling up her wrist and beyond until it encased her entire arm in jagged crystal. And then, the moment it hardened, it exploded. Lees slid backward awkwardly before managing to plant her feet and shift her weight to press against the rapidly expanding Hyper column.

Red Hyper crashed into the yellow Hyper of the Enforcer's hammer, halting its deadly arc right above Lees' head. Their combined force kicked up an unnatural wind, and Lees narrowed her eyes against the grit flying in her face. Something crunched in the back of her mouth.

The two shapers stood frozen, the world around them filled with an uneasy silence. Sweat dripped down Lees' back and forehead as she strained to hold position. One bead rolled down her brow, carving a path through the grime to the corner of her eye. The scene around her swayed in a moment of lightheadedness, and she tried not to gasp for breath while it righted itself.

At any moment, the standstill could break. Either of their concentrations could shatter. She had to make sure it wasn't hers that faltered first. Though only vaguely aware of where he was, Lees knew Teeg was still nearby, hurt and vulnerable.

At first, she thought a fire was roaring in the buildings nearby, and her heart sank. But slowly the sounds came together in her chaotic mind, and she realized – they were cheering.

Shouts of excitement and rallying cries grew louder around them. The residents of Last Light had seen what happened, had watched a mite, one of theirs, stand up to this outside force with such a spectacular display of skill. Lees' heart swelled in her chest at the sound.

"Not bad," The Enforcer commented through gritted teeth.

"Too proud to admit you're struggling?" Lees jeered in what even she knew was a ridiculous surge of confidence. But she couldn't help it. People were cheering. For her.

"Hardly," The Enforcer scoffed. Without easing the force pressed against Lees' Hyper pillar, he twisted his hips to swiftly kick the back of her legs. Her knees buckled.

Lees didn't want to hit the ground. She'd be squished like a bug, ground into paste by the mammoth hammer. The Hyper Object seemed to agree. Some of the crystalized Hyper around her shoulder split off to catch her before her head connected with the cobblestone.

Down came the hammer again. Lees rolled out of the way before aiming another pillar of Hyper at his exposed side. For a second, nothing happened, and Lees desperately tried to conjure an image of what she wanted. A voice she couldn't recognize burst into laughter somewhere near the back of her skull. Jagged spikes of Hyper exploded from her hand and struck the Enforcer near his kidneys, hitting sturdy armor but still sending him flying into a nearby wall. His back connected with the building's brick exterior, and he crumpled to the ground.

Lees goggled at her arm in surprise. The sharp stone rolled over itself in her clenched fist like a warm mass of writhing worms.

Why does this feel easier? She wondered.

BOOOOOMMMMMM!

Another explosion, this time from near the third tier. Townspeople poured out of the smoke-filled buildings into the streets, coughing and gagging, injured and covered in debris. Teeg looked desperately between the new cloud of smoke and back at Lees.

"It's not safe," Lees said.

Ike appeared above her, and Lees let herself be pulled back to her feet. Like scuttling crabs, the slabs of Hyper covering her body retreated into the object safely nestled in her palm.

"We can handle this from here," Ike assured Teeg. The talented mechanic kept his eyes pinned on Lees, unwilling or unable to look away. A few bricks tumbled away from the Enforcer-shaped crater in the wall.

"Go!" Lees shouted. It was enough to shake him out of the trance. Teeg nodded reluctantly before jogging toward the fires.

"Pathetic! Get up, you asshole!" Meshi screamed at the Enforcer lying prone against the damaged side of the apartment block. He stomped his foot before kicking dust at him.

The Enforcer shot out of the rubble and grabbed Meshi, who squealed in surprise. With one hand, the Enforcer shoved a chunk of concrete off his leg, keeping his other hand wrapped around Meshi's throat. He pulled the boy's face down to his level before throwing him to the side.

Lees' stomach turned at the strangled whimper Meshi made when he landed.

Seemingly in response to this disgust, images whipped through Lees' mind in a frenzied stream – *stabbing him, crushing him, anything to put him down and get away.* Through the haze of violence, Lees could make out the Enforcer standing to his full height and barreling toward her once again. *Prying the armor off with surgical precision, eviscerating his exposed body, slashing him to pieces.*

Ike noticed Lees' sudden slack face and unfocused eyes, as if she were trying to shake something loose in her mind.

"Focus! Don't let it consume you!" He shouted, leaping forward to grab her shoulder. But shaking her wasn't helping.

Lees could hear Ike yelling. She could see the Enforcer charging like a mad bull towards her. But she was powerless against the thoughts surging through her brain. She couldn't picture anything clearly through the cluttered visions, couldn't think straight to sort them out. All she could do was scream against the intrusion in her mind.

Shield!

The world beyond was shrouded in fog, a hazy backdrop against the flood of panicked ideas that weren't hers. Somewhere close by, the Enforcer's arm pulled back.

Shield! Shield! SHIELD!

The furious, Hyper-sheathed fist of the Enforcer flew through the air, threatening to shatter Lees' unprotected face. The Hyper Object burst from her hand. Thick bands of Hyper flew out in a spiral pattern, swirling around her arm to form a rigid, glowing shield.

Again, violent winds flared from the spot where Hyper connected with Hyper. Rubble from the Enforcer's collision with the building flew through the air, striking Ike and Meshi.

Meshi cackled as the Enforcer bore down with all of his weight. Lees absorbed the force as best as she could before pushing back against him.

"Give it up, mite!" Meshi spat. A dark bruise was already forming across his throat from where he'd been thrown. Lees grimaced at the sight. Ike stalked over to the boy.

The Enforcer lifted the lion's head once more in his free hand and smashed it into Lees' shield. He bashed it over and over again, each blow knocking her further back. With each strike, he growled, "You. Are. *Nothing.*"

While every ounce of physical strength was put into keeping the shield intact, Lees was mentally elsewhere. She argued desperately with the Hyper Object in her mind.

Please, you were just working so well! We can beat him! Let me think!

She could sense the rising panic in the Hyper Object as the visions became more frenetic and violent. Bloody bodies, blazing fires, and imploding buildings flooded her mind, each more rapid than the last, until the edges of her vision darkened. The shield was destabilizing with every new hit from the hammer.

"Would you just shut up!?" Lees screamed at the Enforcer. Then, as much to the Hyper Object as herself, she muttered, "Please, just concentrate. You need to focus."

BOOOOOOMMMMMMM!

Another massive explosion rocked the town from somewhere on the south side. Centralized warning sirens kicked on, their low wailing punctuated by a fresh wave of screams.

Lees' breath caught in her throat. She blinked back the sudden stinging in her eyes. People were getting hurt, maybe her fellow miners and friends, and there was nothing she could do to stop it.

Her concentration wavered, and the Hyper shield protecting her shattered just as the Enforcer took a full-bodied swing at her. Lees' vision went black when the lion's open mouth connected with her jaw. Something cracked, and her mouth filled with the sharp metallic taste of her own blood. Searing pain erased all thoughts and visions, narrowing her world to a series of sensations: throat tightening, bile rising, head throbbing, ears ringing.

Time stopped as she lay crumpled on the ground.

With one eye cracked open, Lees watched the Enforcer

step back to readjust his gilded helm. He looked around with satisfaction at the plumes of smoke in the distance, so thick now they could taste it in the air. There was a forced cockiness in his stance, but through the pain, Lees noticed he was keeping a careful distance and breathing hard.

"You really thought you had me on the ropes, eh?" The Enforcer was making a show of adjusting his gauntlet, flicking minuscule debris from its golden plates. He rested the hammer next to him and continued unnecessarily adjusting his armor. "No, you see, I'm just getting started."

Thoughts crawled through the pain-induced fog in her brain.

Beneath her, erratic vibrations buzzed through her body and sent shivers down her spine. Lees' chest tightened in panic – *was this some great power of his? Was he really holding back that much?* - but no, this wasn't him. The Enforcer was still admiring the destruction around him. Tiny pinpricks dug into her palm, offering an unusual grounding effect that dulled the pain in her jaw. Lees wrapped her other hand around the Hyper Object and held it tightly. Its buzzing slowed.

You're not afraid, Lees told herself, willing it to be true. *You're going to be okay.*

Pleased with his squire's handiwork, the Enforcer finally returned his attention to Lees. He smiled cruelly at her bleeding and twisted form, and stretched out his shoulders before gripping the handle of the lion hammer once more. He slung it over his shoulder and, without warning, leapt forward to crush her.

There was no time to react. There was no time to *think*. Lees drew the Hyper Object closer to her chest to protect it from what would surely be a near-fatal hit.

Arms gripped her torso and hoisted her upward like a rag doll. She barely had time to register what was happening. The Enforcer's hammer smacked the ground right next to her leg in a shower of bright yellow sparks, and the unnatural tremors from the impact nearly tripped the enormous man carrying her to safety.

Well, relative safety. Lees could see the Enforcer watching her and her protector vanish down a side street. He stayed partially crouched from the attack, hands still wrapped around the hammer, with a look that betrayed neither anger nor worry.

"You good?" Ike asked breathlessly. Lees pressed her back against the wall to stand on shaky legs opposite him. Blood soaked his shirt where the wounds from his fight with Meshi had reopened.

Lees looked at the Hyper Object, at its edges stained pink from where it dug into her hand. Her legs finally gave out, and she sank to a crouch against the alley wall.

"No," She whispered. Though muted, they could still hear the shouts of people fleeing from the chaos. Tears blurred her vision. "Ike, I-I can't do this."

CRACK-BOOOM!

Buildings were collapsing now. Stonework cracked from the force of explosions and crumbled to the ground. Another wave of screaming filled the air.

"Look at them scatter like cockroaches. It didn't have to come to this, you know," The Enforcer bellowed. Either he knew where they were and was toying with her, or he hoped to goad her into revealing their location. Her heart hammered in her chest, pumping fear through her veins to every corner of her existence.

The Hyper Object quivered on her open palm, glowing faintly as it heated up. Fresh visions danced to life in the corner of her mind again.

"Focus!" Ike snapped. He grabbed her shoulders tightly. "You have to learn to control it. When we get back out there—"

"When!?" Lees whimpered. Her voice cracked.

"Yes. When. You *can* do this, Lees. You have to do this," Ike shook her a little too forcefully. Nausea swirled in her gut, and her mouth watered. She swallowed hard, willing herself not to puke on Ike's boots.

"You *can*," Ike repeated. "Keep your thoughts on a singular shape. The simpler the better. You can't let yourself be distracted."

Lees nodded.

"He's a big guy, so you're gonna need to get creative. Focus on speed, remember? You're faster and lighter. Find a way to knock him down and get that hammer away from him."

"He's too strong, I can't do that, I don't know what to do," Lees stammered.

"I'm growing bored of this game, little girl," The Enforcer taunted. Lees flinched.

"Focus. Think about it, why isn't he chasing us down this alley right now? Why is he standing in the square shouting at us? He saw where we went. He's not even expending the energy to hunt us down," Ike said.

"He's over-confident," Lees puzzled. Ike nodded emphatically.

"If he underestimates you, let him," Ike encouraged with a wink. Was that excitement in his eyes? *Do all cutlass enjoy fighting so much that they lose all sense?* Lees' stomach turned again, but maybe he was right.

"He's banking on you being afraid of him. Fear makes people stupid and slow. Don't give him that power," Ike continued. His eyes darted to either end of the alley, assessing the best way out or maybe checking for trouble. Lees was still on the ground, and he'd basically been huddling over her the entire time they'd been there, leaving his back exposed. Reckless to the point of unprofessionalism for a trained cutlass.

Is he itching to rejoin the fight? Lees wondered.

Ike bobbed his head, and Lees realized he was making a nervous clicking sound with his tongue as he looked around, head tilted to listen. He remained crouched, hands on her shoulders, the position designed to shield her from whatever might come at them.

No, this wasn't excitement or a love of fighting. That wasn't what compelled him.

What was it he'd said to her down in the bunker? *There's something special about you. The Hyper Object has a reason for choosing you. You're the most powerful Seer in the world.*

The tension in her core eased, and a smile crept across Lees' face despite the situation. She unclenched her jaw and used Ike's shoulders to pull herself up.

"Okay," Lees wiped her mouth, wincing at the sharp prickling along her gum line.

"Oh," Ike said in surprise when Lees wrapped her arms around him to give a slightly painful hug.

He squeezed her gently. "All right, kid, let's do this."

"We got this," Lees whispered to the stone. When she wrapped her fingers around it this time, the Hyper Object felt cooler, more stable somehow. It reminded her of an ice pack – she'd kill for one right now, but this isn't the time; she needed to focus.

Lees took a shaky step, then another, and another. Each time her foot connected with the ground, the stabbing pain in her side and jaw peeled away one layer at a time. By the time she stepped out of the shadowed alley and into the yellow light, everything that had been hurting was somehow reduced to nothing more than a dull ache.

Focus, she told herself. *Keep your eyes on your enemy. Think about what will counter him.*

The Enforcer still stood in the center of the square, leaning against his hammer. He watched her without making a move.

"Aw, did I make you angry? I hope you're not mad at me," He jeered. Lees glared at him but stood her ground. The Enforcer swung the hammer in an arc until it rested across his back before casually striding her way.

"We do this together. Keep your distance and support me when I strike him up close. You ready?" Ike whispered. Lees gave him a most unconvincing smile, but Ike accepted it all the same.

Ike lunged forward with an agility she didn't expect. The Enforcer seemed to be caught off guard as well, fumbling as the cutlass caught him off balance. With surprising grace, Ike dodged the knight's sweeping open-handed strike and sank his elbow into the front of the Enforcer's exposed neck. Ike levered his elbow upward against his trachea to snap his head back, knocking the stupid ornate helmet to the ground.

This was the moment Ike was setting up for her. He'd put himself in direct harm to give her a shot at hitting this guy.

Lees' thoughts spun. She needed a weapon, something that could hit the Enforcer with enough force to knock him over, golden armor and all. Something that could reach him from where she stood and drag his feet out from under him. Distance, force, strength. Like racing through a mental catalog, her thoughts whipped through her options until she narrowed on an idea. The stone's now-familiar vibration acti-vated as if answering her call.

The Hyper Object oozed out from the gaps between her fingers, once again enveloping Lees' arm in its beautiful, vicious coating. Pulsating red and warm against her skin. From her palm, a thin, flexible strand of unbreakable Hyper extended out and out in a seemingly endless rope, tighten-ing into a whip that snapped straight back at the Enforcer.

Ike instinctively jumped out of the path of Lees' attack. She willed herself to narrow her focus on the Enforcer and him alone. Nothing else mattered right now.

Lees' Hyper whip struck and retracted in a high arc with lightning speed and impossible precision, slashing the Enforcer's exposed face and neck again and again. His hammer fell to the ground with a thunderous boom to free his hands to protect his head, but Lees' Hyper wouldn't be deterred that easily. The shimmering whip wrapped itself around one wrist and wrenched it back, leaving his head vul-nerable again. With a sensation of a ligament being plucked like a cord, a second Hyper whip strand burst from her palm and left a vicious gash across the Enforcer's face.

He grunted in pain with each fresh attack. The whip showed no signs of breaking or slowing as it pushed him further back, away from her and Ike. Her plan was wildly suc-cessful, but there was a problem. The dual Hyper whip was much harder to control than the stagnant shield. It almost had a mind of its own. Lees gripped the oozing Hyper in her fist with both hands now, struggling to maintain the shape.

One of the whips faltered and then snapped upward in an uncontrollable arc. The Enforcer snatched up his weapon and swung it sideways, knocking back each repeated attack with brutal force. Yellow Hyper surged from his shoulder into the hammer, adding to the thickness of its handle and strengthening the screaming lion.

Lees narrowed her focus further on the dual whip. Immediately, the connection snapped back into place. She was surprised by how sturdy the Hyper Object's extension felt. Each whip's slender shape was dwarfed by the massive hammer, as fragile as a twig ready to snap at any moment. But neither did. Though she felt every blow in her core as it rumbled down the length of the whips, both strands repelled every strike from the Enforcer.

Again and again, the frenzied whips tore through the air and struck the Enforcer from every angle.

It felt... good. *She could do this.* Lees closed her eyes, channeling her breathing to match the Hyper Object's pulses, thinking of the whip as an extension of her own body. The Hyper whip ceased its chaotic thrashing against the Enforcer and hung steadfast in the air above him. She imagined the Enforcer losing balance, then replayed the visual in her mind.

Finally, Lees opened her eyes and smirked. *So, this was what it was like to have power.* She took a heavy step forward, steadied herself, then another step. Violence raced through her mind, spurred by either her own desires or the Hyper Object's bloodthirst, or perhaps both.

This is the man who brought destruction to her town. This is the man who tried to destroy her home.

This is the man who made Teeg bleed.

The Enforcer was undeterred by this sudden shift, returning her look with a sinister smile. With the whips slowed, he took the opportunity to step closer to her. Ike took a running leap and wrapped himself around the Enforcer's hammer-wielding arm.

"Lees! Do it now!" Ike yelled. He bucked his hips to pull the Enforcer's arm up to expose his side, summoning every ounce of strength to fight against him.

There was no time to hesitate. Lees closed the gap and sent the suspended Hyper strands flying into the Enforcer's chest.

Bits and pieces of the golden armor snapped away. Each end of the Hyper whips split in two, forming gaping maws flanked by razor-sharp sets of teeth. These snapping serpent heads intertwined into a precision strike aimed at the newly weakened spot on the armor. Larger scales flew from the armor, exposing a soft, latticework layer below.

The Enforcer's smile was replaced by a look that betrayed his true feelings. His eyes darted between Ike, Lees, and the twin Hyper strands, calculating his best chances for survival while his sturdy, ornate armor was torn apart by these viper strikes.

He finally turned his body and raised a free arm to block the whip attack, but any attempt to stop her was in vain. Lees was consumed by the surging power that drove her dual serpents to assault every inch of his exposed body. Each whip strike held the armor in place, allowing the razor-sharp mouths to snap and tear at its weak points. With each step she took, the jagged snake-like extensions of Hyper lunged forward and then retracted, waiting for the next step. The next opportunity to inflict pain.

Lees' vision went red, but she was still in control. She could feel everything. She was aware of the minuscule weight of the Hyper extending from her arm. She experienced every movement of the whips as they consumed the golden armor. She was careful to make minor adjustments, send little mental reminders, to keep the strands from piercing Ike as he held fast to the Enforcer's arm. The Hyper Object and Lees were resonating perfectly with each other. She would think it, the object would perform it. They were driving toward the same goal, single-minded in their pursuit.

The Enforcer couldn't defend against the never-ending assault with Ike on his back, but he couldn't pry the man off without opening himself up to worse. Strike after strike landed on and around the knight with a speed and ferocity he'd never thought was possible with Hyper.

"WHAT ARE YOU DOING!?" Meshi's voice wormed its way through Lees' concentration. She had forgotten he was even here. "She's nothing! A worthless little novice who doesn't even know how to shape! You're the goddamn Enforcer! Use your Hyper and pulverize her already!"

Meshi's whiny, screeching insults had as much of an effect on the Enforcer as they did on Lees. He roared in frustration and desperation, and her twin whip attack stuttered. That was all the Enforcer needed. Yellow Hyper tendrils seethed from the exposed sections of his armor. Two prongs shot up from where Ike clung to him, loosening his grip. Those prongs immediately twisted around Ike's midsection and launched him away.

Lees cringed when Ike hit the ground, but pushed herself to stay focused on the Enforcer. *Now is not the time.* Her whips redoubled their work, striking at him again and again. But the yellow Hyper was distracting – it moved so fluidly, as if an extension not just of the Enforcer's body but of his fury. The strands of Hyper from her own hand slowed.

NO! We're almost there! I just have to bring him down! Don't stop! Lees screamed.

The Hyper whips pulsed out of rhythm and struck the knight's legs a dozen times in succession. One curled at the last second, hitting him squarely in the back of the knee. The Enforcer's leg collapsed, but before his knee could touch the ground, a clump of murky yellow Hyper spiraled down his leg and through the holes in his armor to anchor him to the ground.

Lees took a deep breath and pulled the whips around for what might be a final attack.

Blazing Hyper strands erupted from the Enforcer's torso. Lees' dual whips frantically changed course to intercept them and protect her face, but that wasn't their target. Two strands tightened into small rods as they barreled toward Lees' hand holding the Hyper Object. She flexed her hand, but she couldn't move – each of her whips was now tangled in a writhing mass of yellow Hyper tendrils.

Lees tried pulling the whips free, directing the serpent mouths to snap the strands apart, but it was no use. She was trapped, and retracting the whip strands would only bring the yellow Hyper closer to the Hyper Object.

The Enforcer watched Lees' fruitless struggle with a determined grin before viciously yanking on his own Hyper strands to pull in the ensnared whips. Lees was pulled along with them. She lost her balance being dragged to the Enforcer, feeling her advantage slip the closer she got. Dozens more tendrils oozed from his shoulders to smack Lees into the ground and hold her there.

Whatever had been dulling the pain from before ceased. The agony of her likely broken jaw and cracked ribs consumed her in an instant. Her ears rang shrilly, and the world danced around her.

A vision of her dropping the Hyper Object blared in her mind, loud and shrill like a train whistle, repeating over and over. She must have let go at some point, and it fell noiselessly to the ground. Something rumbled beneath her, slowly at first, then building into a violent earthquake that rocked her head up and back down. It felt like the blast had happened inside her body, scrambling her lungs and stomach. Her mind went blank. The ground was cold beneath her temple. It was almost soothing. But then something was disturbing the air around her, a frantic motion. People running. People panicking.

Lees squinted. Orange-black smoke and fire filled the square. A whooshing sound echoed in her ears, then more rumbling like falling rocks. Smoking debris began falling around the square – wooden splinters, superheated metal, fractured stones. Was this real? *Am I awake?*

She could barely breathe now, so thick was the ash and smoke. A golden glimmer drew her attention up to see the Enforcer limping over, his face shielded once again by the ornate helmet. Its ferocious leonine face loomed closer until it eclipsed her view.

An acrid, acidic smell burned her nostrils. It clicked into place, just as she was losing consciousness.

"The mine," She mouthed. And then everything went dark.

CHAPTER 14

Desperate Measures

The mine had exploded. Ka-boom. Destroyed. Gone. Their livelihood, Last Light's purpose, now up in smoke and flames. Disintegrated by the interlopers, those thugs in armor surging through the tiers of the city like a plague to destroy everything they'd worked for.

Plumes of acrid smoke rose through the layers of Last Light, swirling around the Rapidite node and nearly blotting out its pale yellow light.

One face of a high-rise apartment complex near the mine had been blasted away. Chunks of concrete and broken furniture sprawled across the street below.

Every window in a quarter-mile radius shattered in the explosion. People will be finding shards in unexpected places for weeks. Replacing the glass would be a nightmare if they even bothered. Without the mine, what did they have left?

Roaring fire raging from deep beyond the mine entrance drowned out everything else.

But there was no way for Lees to actually know any of this. She still lay where she'd fallen with her bruised eyes squeezed shut, brain sluggishly bubbling beneath its blanket of semi-consciousness. Sounds, thoughts, and sensations surfaced and disappeared.

Visions, she thought vaguely. *But why?*

Someone had arrived. It must be one of the Enforcer's squires returning without his helmet, but his face was blurry for some reason as he charged across the square. Targeting someone. Targeting her.

Why show me this?

He held up a mace with a glowing end, such a strange weapon for him to wield, and Lees watched him get closer and closer, closing the distance to reach her – and then bands of red crystal snapped around her like a ribcage, protecting her and throwing him backward.

"LEES!"

A voice pierced through the fog and nudged her wandering thoughts into place. Ike. The square. The Enforcer. The fire. Sirens bellowed from all directions, and waves of heat rolled over her.

Lees wrenched open her eyes in time to catch four Hyper spikes retreating into her hand. She hadn't dropped the stone after all. As her eyes adjusted, they fell on Meshi, who was hunched over and cradling his arm, groaning in frustrated pain.

She scooted back on instinct.

"Dangerous even when knocked out. Interesting. Glad it caught him and not me."

The Enforcer was suddenly right above her, his voice low and infuriatingly calm, like he wasn't affected at all from his recent meeting with a brick wall or the teeth-rattling catastrophe below them. His heavy-topped hammer tilted over her head, yellow Hyper practically leaping from that snarling mouth. Lees locked eyes with him through the ridiculous helmet, trying to keep Meshi in her peripheral vision without breaking eye contact with the Enforcer. They were both dangerous, but only one of them was in a position to kill her right now.

"Lees! Move!" Ike screamed. His voice was getting louder. Lees widened her eyes in a wild attempt to expand her field of vision, and a tiny movie of him sprinting toward them played in her head.

"There's no need for you to die too, fool," The Enforcer said. He looked away from Lees, and she rolled out of the way. Ike must have continued running for them, because the Enforcer clicked his tongue and snarled, "You miners are too stupid to learn your lesson the first few times? Fine. Let's get this over with."

Lees eyed the hammer, but the Enforcer raised his fist

instead. Hyper shot out of the holes in his armor in a torrent to form two dinner plate-sized columns targeting Ike's chest. The cutlass smiled – actually *smiled* at the move – and jumped into the air. Ike landed on one column, then the other, knocking them off course and sending them crashing to the ground. The Enforcer stumbled forward as the weight shifted, and Ike leaned his shoulder into a bone-crunching punch that would have leveled an ordinary man.

The gilded armor rattled with the force of the Enforcer's Hyper being dragged back through its channels. Lees was on her knees now, waiting for the square to stop spinning before getting to her feet. Ike stepped back nimbly, arms up and ready for the counterattack. His gaze snapped to hers for a moment, and he jerked his head to the alley they'd come from. She nodded.

Meshi lay curled in a ball on the ground near Ike. He was making no effort to stop her or help the Enforcer or do anything except whimper. Lees turned to make a break for it.

"You stay put until I'm done here," The Enforcer snapped. Lightning fast, a yellow tendril sailed through the air and pierced her shoulder. Sharp coldness bloomed across her chest where the tendril neatly passed through skin and between bone before burying itself into the ground below, pinning her in place.

Lees had never been cut or stabbed by Hyper until today. The feeling was staticky with a fluctuating energy that moved in an utterly horrible, grotesque way. An alien heartbeat just out of sync with her own. It felt *wrong,* somehow, and in the throes of that painful feeling, she thought that the Hyper seemed apologetic for what was happening.

She was pinned on her back with the fight out of view. All she could see was Meshi staring at her predicament with a mixture of unabashed disgust and satisfaction. He crawled toward her gracelessly, shooting furtive glances to where she could hear Ike and the Enforcer exchanging blows, and nearly lost balance when he reached her side.

"No-!" She whispered, choking on the words before she could finish. Nothing vital was punctured or damaged, but the Enforcer's Hyper spear seemed to have momentarily paralyzed her. Meshi tore at her hand, a frantic but familiar move that brought her back to the cave during their first fight. Try as she might, Lees couldn't get the exhausted muscles in her arm to cooperate. It didn't take long for Meshi to pry open her fingers and wrap his own around the stone.

Fear forgotten, Meshi scuttled to the side and held his prize high, cackling with joy, simultaneously a greedy child and haughty upper-crust elite in his celebration.

It was like her heart had been ripped from her. Lees screamed and writhed against her captor even as the Hyper tendril piercing her shoulder sent electric sparks along her veins. The Hyper Object's absence tore open a chasm of grief, a loss so profound she could feel it in her bone marrow.

Her scream reached a pitch that tore her throat. Ike shifted his attention to her, an understandable but foolish miscalculation, and the Enforcer pounced on it. He snaked a vine of Hyper around the cutlass' neck and flung him into the crumpled wall at the far end of the square.

"Stop getting back up!" He commanded before rounding on Meshi. The boy shook his clenched fist above his head, then cradled it close to his chest, all the while still laughing uncontrollably. "Well, now. Good for you, little prince. You got your stone, and all it took was the complete destruction of this entire mining outfit."

"You won't be so smug when you see what I can do with it," Meshi sneered.

"I'm sure I will be very impressed," The Enforcer replied dryly.

The Enforcer relaxed his stance and massaged one shoulder through the armor. He looked around the square and did a double-take at Lees, as if noticing for the first time that she was pinned. He drew the tendril back, taking care to do so as slowly as possible until it was clear of her shoulder. She gasped. "Goodness, but that looked painful. I have to admit, I'm genuinely impressed. You're a resilient bunch. That won't save you in the end, but I commend you for it."

The Enforcer's words stirred a fiery desire for vengeance, but that feeling was nothing compared to the longing raging in her chest that demanded she tear Meshi apart for what he stole. He looked so happy, so crazed in his joy, that Lees could think of nothing else but ripping it away from him.

Brutal violence bore down on her: Meshi's face swollen

beyond the point of recognition and a battered pile of golden armor ablaze in the streets. This new wave of visions was distant and muted compared to the others. Lees could still see around them, and her thoughts were still there, distinct from the Hyper Object's.

Do the visions fade when it has a new owner?

Lees could only manage to roll over. Grit still coated her mouth. She could feel it gathering on the inside of her cheeks and grinding between her teeth, collecting in her lungs with each ragged breath. Lees pressed against the wound on her shoulder and gasped. Her coat, the gift from Teeg, a precious memento from his past, had been torn and stained with her blood.

His act of kindness, ruined.

"*Hold on,*" The strained voice of Ike rose out of the rubble. But he wasn't moving.

Orange-hued smoke was everywhere now. The Enforcer pulled a mask over his mouth and nose. Meshi's breath sank into a wheeze between fits of laughter. For the first time since the alarm had sounded, Lees looked around at her town. The Hyper Object had shown her visions of the explosion's aftermath, but the reality was somehow grimmer. There wasn't a soul around, but she could hear her fellow townspeople's shouts in the distance. Broken glass glittered on the ground. Ripples of heat shimmered around them from the fires that must be deep inside the mine. It could burn for days, weeks, maybe even months.

Can one piece of Hyper really be worth all this? She wondered.

A tug in her chest pulled her eyes back to the fist clenched around the Hyper Object demanding her attention. But like the last set of visions, this pang was weak. Easy to shrug off, if she wanted.

If the Enforcer secures the stone, would they all leave? Would Last Light be safe?

"Just go," Lees whispered. The Enforcer looked down at her with amusement. Flipbook-style images flitted across her eyes: the Enforcer's face coated in blood, grinning widely as he brought the hammer down on innocent civilians in his path. Then back to his current state. Over and over.

It was too much.

"Please," Lees said softly. "Leave. Go."

Nausea gripped her insides. She doubled over where she sat, fighting the urge to throw up. More insistent and vivid than before, Lees was flooded with images: Her mother clutching her limp body. Teeg laying flowers at her grave. Jez laying flowers at Teeg's grave. Her own lifeless eyes staring up at a smoke-filled sky.

Lees took a deep, rattling breath and let them play out. The Hyper Object was desperate and in the throes of a final temper tantrum. Throwing everything it could at her. But what in the world could she possibly do?

"Are you managing all right there, boy?" The Enforcer asked. Meshi growled in response. Both hands were wrapped around the Hyper Object, which was vibrating wildly out of control. Angry red light dripped between his fingers as he smothered it against his chest.

The Hyper Object wasn't even cooperating with him. Did Meshi realize he couldn't wield it even if he wanted to? Did that power belong to her?

"Kill her," He spat. The Enforcer looked surprised.

"You got your rock, didn't you? That doesn't seem very sportsmanlike."

Lees glared at Meshi. Her staggered breathing matched the Hyper Object's pulsing rhythm in his hands.

"I'll double your fee," Meshi said. The longer Lees looked at him, the greater her hatred grew. True, the Enforcer had triggered most of this destruction himself, but this upper crest boy had infiltrated her town, manipulated the people she cared about, and taken advantage of their kindness. He didn't deserve that power. He didn't deserve to have it all turn out well for him in the end.

"The Royal Oppri Assembly and its associates compensate me quite well, thank you," The Enforcer said haughtily. Something rumbled nearby - the briefest sound of shifting stone - but then it stopped.

"That's not the kind of fee I meant," Meshi replied, then let out a muffled cry of frustration. He turned away from Lees, inadvertently turning his back on the Enforcer, and staggered to the partially destroyed train platform stairs.

Over his shoulder, he said, "Do it fast and call your men back. We need to leave."

It might not be worth the trouble. It might have destroyed Last Light. But he can't have it.

Silent pleas radiated from the stone. Lees rose to her knees, mentally reaching out, but her body didn't have the strength left to do what it needed to do.

The Enforcer clicked his tongue at Meshi's retreating form, then sighed as he picked up the lion-head hammer once more.

"Sorry, kid, but he makes a compelling offer," The Enforcer said. The sound of the hammer scraping along the ground made Lees' ears ache. "For what it's worth, you're much braver than most I'm sent after to correct. And if it's any consolation, I truly hate destroying anything useful. Your shaping is exceptional. It's a pity, really."

Lees scrambled back, but even with how slow the Enforcer was walking, there was no way she was getting away from him with these injuries. With every step he took, fear squeezed her heart tighter. Regret flung itself around her chest, bitter and chilling, as the reality of the situation dawned on her.

This man was going to kill her, and she had lost the one thing that could stop him.

When Lees had reported for her first shift and rode down the mine shaft for the first time, she was petrified. Staring down into the howling maw of darkness and suffocating closeness, she began hyperventilating before they'd gone

100 feet down. After the hundredth shift or so, that feeling of being trapped without an escape had eased enough to allow her to get the job done. But on the nights she wasn't haunted by the memory of chippers on her twentieth birthday, nightmares of the deep tormented her. Terror overtakes her senses in those moments, and whether asleep in her bed or exhausted after a shift, her mind is only soothed by the pinpoint of light that grows larger and brighter as the lift ascends back to safety.

The Enforcer's shadow eclipsed her. His silhouette of golden armor and lion-head hammer blocked out the light, and that cloying, claustrophobic fear bubbled to the surface. Pinned. Trapped. Out of options.

What about when he kills you? she asked herself. *Will he send backup to take out the protesters? Would he send people to level the town, finish the job?*

Yellow Hyper flared from seemingly every pore on his gilded armor, its glow adding a sickly gauntness to the Enforcer's broad face. Deep shadows formed beneath his eyes from the light. Murderous though his intentions might be, he wasn't smiling like she'd expected, like the Hyper Object had depicted him in its panicked flurry of visions. He was hesitating.

"Aren't you going to try to run?" He muttered.

Was he...trying to help her?

"Lees, run!" Her thoughts were interrupted by Ike, who had managed to free himself during the brief break in action.

The Enforcer must not have noticed him either, because Ike was able to latch himself onto the imposing man's neck and yank him sideways. The two men struggled but remained standing.

RUN! Lees screamed at herself, but her legs wouldn't move.

She flinched, expecting another onslaught of visions predicting the outcome of this latest fight, but her mind was strangely silent. Expecting relief, Lees was surprised to find she was disappointed. With how hard it'd fought to reach her, why wasn't it putting up more of a fight now?

The Enforcer dropped the hammer and grabbed Ike with both hands, bent low, and flipped him over his armored shoulder to the ground. Ike hit the ground hard. He rounded on Lees once more, this time his eyes blazing with resolve, all hesitation gone.

This was her last chance. There was nothing left to do except...

Lees squeezed her eyes shut and willed herself to make contact with the Hyper Object. Everything she'd said about it, denying its connection, fearing its violence, hating it for making her hurt Jcz, came rushing back.

I'm sorry. I'm sorry, but please, I need your help. I need you, she thought, imagining the unspoken words flowing along an invisible thread to wherever Meshi had fled. Her fingers twitched with the memory of rolling the stone along her palm. Though she'd never controlled it before, she willed herself to be back in the crystal void, searching through her mind for the disembodied hand. *I will be your Seer. I will be your vessel. Please.*

Lees helped this stranger wake the Hyper Object, bringing all of this down on her town. She was responsible for the wreckage, for the injuries, for the destroyed mine. Whatever it took, whatever she had to do, it would be worth it to make up for what she'd done.

What would she become? Did it even matter anymore, so long as she could protect her people?

A bright red droplet fell to the ground between her knees. She heard it hit with a deafening sound before a shockwave vibrated outward. With each ripple, she watched a scowling Meshi leave Last Light empty-handed. Her mining crew temporarily on leave to sift through debris in the square to rebuild it better than before. Teeg clinking a glass of vinium against Jez's tumbler of rotgut after hours at the Eye of Mite. Jez pulling Lees in for an embrace so passionate that it made their previous kiss seem chaste.

She shuddered with the emotional swirl of these moments. She deserved to see them come true. To live in this world. Something blossomed deep in her, a sudden sense of belonging. Of being wanted.

When Lees finally opened her eyes, the Enforcer stopped in his tracks. Her eyes were clouded over with rapidly shifting colors, the pupils, irises, and whites completely overtaken.

"What is this?" The Enforcer asked.

Meshi's shriek could be heard blocks away. His hands, still clasped around the stone, had been eviscerated by needlelike points of Hyper erupting through his skin. The boy wobbled on his feet, his eyes drooping and his face a pale mask of horror, as hundreds of Hyper barbs expanded farther and farther. Even if he wanted to let go, his hands were literally anchored in place.

Lees reached out her hand, feeling but not seeing.

With a metallic *shk-ink!* the needles sucked back into the stone in Meshi's hands. He ripped what was left of his palms apart and screamed at the carnage.

The Hyper Object, now so small and innocent-looking, fell from his grip, picking up speed and rocketing toward Lees and the Enforcer without touching the ground. Through the chaotic swirling that obscured her vision, a pinpoint of light pierced through, steadily growing, beckoning her out of the suffocating darkness.

Lees snatched the projectile out of the air without much effort. Before it hit her skin, it pooled and oozed around her fingers and wrist, caressing her skin in an embrace before reforming.

She picked it up with her other hand and placed it on her tongue, feeling it smooth its edges before she swallowed it whole.

No - wait, she *saw* herself swallowing it. Lees felt the urge stronger than any the Hyper Object had given her before. The vision played over and over in stunning detail, blocking her senses to everything but this singular desire.

Picking up the Hyper Object. Putting it in my mouth. Swallowing it whole.

"What is she doing?" The Enforcer's voice squeezed through the gaps in the Hyper Object's visions. The words were instantly drowned out.

Ike studied Lees' clouded eyes and sudden stiff demeanor. The Hyper Object's surface gurgled and bubbled in her hand, and the light it gave off became almost too bright to look at.

Picking up the Hyper Object. Putting it in my mouth. Swallowing it whole.

Over and over, again and again, the same motions played across her eyes. Nothing more to offer, nothing more to sway her, just an endless, deep desire for her to consume it.

"Lees, remember. Focus. Whatever you're planning—"

Picking up the Hyper Object. Putting it in my mouth. Swallowing it whole. Picking up the Hyper Object. Putting it in my mouth. Swallowing it whole. Picking up the Hyper Object —

"Okay. I get it," Lees said. The Enforcer and Ike stood side-by-side, united for a moment by their bewilderment at this strange scene.

She looked from one to the other. She picked up the Hyper Object. Put it in her mouth. And swallowed it whole.

CHAPTER 15

Lees the Monster

Eating a live grenade, that's what it felt like. Miniature explosions of superheated matter followed its trajectory down her esophagus and into her stomach, searing the linings of Lees' internal organs along the way. Her heart painfully pumped boiling blood throughout her body, igniting her veins and sizzling nerve endings. Lees might have doubled over, or collapsed, or hovered a foot off the ground; she had no way of knowing. Every thought and feeling was turned inward, focusing only on the sensation of swallowing the Hyper Object.

Her body felt distant. Lees was vaguely aware that she *was* lying on the ground, or so it felt, aware only of Ike's strong hands holding down her flailing limbs. Her mouth was open, and she was screaming, but not with her own voice. She existed above her body, or maybe below it, several feet from her physical form – sensing rather than seeing what unfolded around her.

Bright yellow flared behind her eyelids. The gilded knight, the Enforcer of the Oppri's will and truth, was reinforcing his holy weapon and armor.

"I know what you are, you puppet," He seethed. "And so now I know what I must do. The sacred duty of my position."

He hefted the hammer with its blazing lion head and full weight of authority from the Oppri. When he spoke, it was with words learned in his earliest days of service, the rites committed by memory that so few uttered in practice.

"As the all-seeing eyes of the Exalted gaze upon me, I cast out the stain of impurity within this cursed object. I cleanse our land of the false prophet Seer and all those who abide by it!"

With every ounce of strength, the Enforcer swung the hammer down on the convulsing body of Lees, the newest mite to Last Light.

All at once, the pain in Lees' body vanished. There was a lingering feeling of something caught in her throat, but besides that, she felt fine. Good, even.

Lees sat up, looked around, and sighed.

"This place, again?" Her voice echoed slightly in the crystalline void. She sat on the cold, hard Hyper surface of this strange room once again, staring up at the enormous crystalline hand.

The hand twitched and melted into a puddle. As a new form emerged from its bubbling depths, the scene changed. A wooden floor clattered out from the puddle, board by board. A series of arching windows bent over her head. A scuffed but clean wooden table stretched out before her. The figure began to take shape, perched on a three-legged stool, shoulders rounded –

"Oh, absolutely not. Not her again. Uh-uh," Lees said. She squeezed her eyes shut and shook her head as if to erase the even momentary image of her old home and her mother. "Try again."

With her eyes still shut, the Hyper's sloshing and slurping sounds were grotesque. She waited until they subsided, then slowly opened one eye. Sunlight filtered into the familiar, cramped workshop, where every surface spilled over with mechanical components, half-finished machinery, and scattered tools. Her shoulders relaxed.

"Better," She said. Something moved at the corner of her eye, and Lees turned uneasily, expecting to come face-to-face with a crystal homunculus in the shape of Teeg. Instead, a bright ball of soft red light hung just below eye level. Its staticky surface gave it a blurry quality, amplified by the fact that it was shifting almost imperceptibly in midair.

Another shape stalked out from behind a standing tool-box, its silky fur catching the light of the afternoon sun. Lees grinned and gently passed a hand over the purt's back. The little creature wound around her outstretched legs and nuzzled against her hip.

"So what's the deal?" Lees said, addressing the ball while petting the purt. "I know I'm not *here* here, like my body is still out…in the real world. Am I safe? Why did you bring me here?"

The ball's surface grew placid. It bobbed up and down, gently at first, but as Lees watched from her seat, its movements became more insistent. Its surface prickled; minuscule spikes emerged and vanished over and over.

Lees stood up, and the workshop pitched around her for a split second. The ball bobbed and moved backward a few inches. When Lees didn't move, it moved back into its original position and then flew backward a bit further.

"Are you trying to show me something?" She asked. Again, the red ball responded only by jerking backward, resetting itself, then doing it again. Lees cocked her head, and the ball suddenly flew forward to smack squarely into her chest. She slammed into a tall set of drawers. A board someone had set precariously on its edge teetered and fell right above her. Without thinking, Lees reached out an arm to protect her face and knocked it away.

Back on the dusty ground near the train station, Lees' eyes snapped open at the same time a column of the purest red Hyper the Enforcer had ever seen erupted from the hole in her shoulder where he'd pinned her. It narrowed to a thin blade at the moment of the hammer's impact, neatly severing it in half. Two enormous pieces crashed to the ground on either side of her, a lion divided, each side permanently separated from the other.

The Enforcer stared in shock, body frozen in place. Those eyes of hers swirled with the same pure red color of the Hyper now coursing through the puppet's body.

"What is this?" He whispered.

In a voice half hers, half not, Lees replied, "This is the end."

On reflex, the Enforcer shot out yellow Hyper in all directions, some tendrils attempting to push his body back while the rest aimed for Lees' most vulnerable areas – head, heart, stomach. Lees lifted her right arm, and viscous Hyper bubbled out of her pores to fortify it until it was nearly as tall as her. Fluid-like red Hyper encased each of the Enforcer's strands and hardened around them.

Lees sat up, and the enormous Hyper appendage holding the Enforcer's yellow Hyper in place hoisted him in the air. With her left hand, Lees sent a Hyper blade singing through the air and buried it to the hilt in the Enforcer's shoulder.

"What...have you...become?" The Enforcer howled.

Lees cocked her head at his expression, a mixture of

disbelief and betrayal, then she savagely pulled the Hyper blade down. It met little resistance as it tore through muscle and bone to sever his arm completely.

The Enforcer and his disembodied arm dangled in the air, the two separated by a few inches, before her Hyper-infused arm released his. The yellow Hyper paled in color as it retreated into the limp arm. Without a shaper, it was rendered inert.

"By the divine, Lees, you did it! I don't know how – that can't be safe – but you pulled it off!" Ike howled in surprise. He hoisted himself off the ground and pointed at a side street past the train station. "You really fooled him with that creepy possession act. You'll have to tell me how you did that with your voice later. And you might want to spit that thing out when we're somewhere safe."

He stopped when he realized she wasn't following. Upon a closer look, he noticed with a start that Lees hadn't sat up at all. When she yanked the Enforcer into the air, tiny Hyper fingers pushed against her back to prop her up. He stared in confusion that merged into concern as four more pieces of Hyper emerged from her arms and legs, followed by more and more, each one pressing out from her skin until it broke through to connect with the ground. Each strand bent at a joint, forming spindly, jellylike legs that together supported her full weight.

"Lees! What are you doing? Stop this!" Ike cried. More than three dozen Hyper legs jittered around her, and he tried in vain to grab her before they lifted Lees' body into the air. Her head fell to the side, limp as a doll, and her mouth hung open. Hyper dribbled over her teeth and out of her mouth in a trickle that grew steadily thicker, coating her body in the same swirling, vicious layer.

Lees pushed the red ball away and angrily got to her feet. She kicked the two pieces of the board away from her.

"What is going on?" She demanded. The red ball bobbed slowly, then darted to the workshop door. Crimson light seeped around its edges, darker and somehow more sinister than the red ball's hue. Lees crossed the workshop, trying to ignore the strange feeling of her skin being pulled and stretched, and put a hand on the doorknob.

The red ball panicked. It shivered in place before rushing to thrust itself between her and the door, gently pressing against her to push her away. Heat poured in around the doorframe in unbearable waves, and Lees backed up.

"Keep the door shut," Lees said, nodding.

A thin strand of Hyper extended from the floating ball, splitting into five equal-sized nubs at its end. Lees grimaced, watching the nubs wriggle unnaturally.

"Is that supposed to be a hand?"

The miniature Hyper hand put its "hand" flat in the air. A red blade sprang from the center of it, and the little nubs grasped its handle. The shape was vaguely like a scimitar she'd seen in a children's book. Lees extended her own hand and felt beads of plasma-like material seeping out of her pores. She watched in wonder as blood-red Hyper poured out to form a scimitar in her hand.

"I can shape in here!?" She asked giddily. Lees looked at the ball with suspicion. Miniature features formed across its surface, scurrying little appendages and a long whip-like tail, followed by four triangular ears. "What's happening to me out there?"

The Hyper beast of Lees shuffled forward. A few feet-like tendrils bumped into Ike and gently but firmly pushed him out of the way. Hyper continuously flowed out of every inch of her body to cover her and strengthen the spindly legs, now numbering too many to count.

Ike could see the monstrosity that was Lees was making its way to the Enforcer, who struggled madly to get to his feet with only one arm.

Six or so of the Hyper legs whipped out to wrap around his leg and pull him toward the beast. Gossamer Hyper strings pulled apart several layers of thick red armor on Lees' chest to reveal a cavernous opening lined with jagged teeth. Rows of thick bands popped out of her spine and formed a ribcage around her midsection not unlike the one that had protected her from Meshi earlier.

"P-please, no, I was a fool to think I could take you on. You are no false prophet. F-forgive me. Please, spare me, and I will spread word of your might to the Oppri," The Enforcer wailed. "I will serve you! I'll throw aside my title and follow your will, anything you desire – p-please!"

Lees made no indication that she could hear his blasphemous prayer. Her head bobbed, and the seemingly endless stream of Hyper from within continued flowing.

Ropes of Hyper wormed their way around his body, constricting snake-like around his remaining arm and legs. His gilded armor buckled under the pressure. They probed at his wound, oozed beneath his helmet, flitted between the seams in his armor to press against his skin. Wrapping tighter and tighter into a gelatinous cocoon, the Hyper held him there for a beat – motionless and unswayed by his pleas and moans.

"Ike? What is this!?" Meshi descended from the platform and hurried to Ike, his hands cradled in his torn shirt, taking solace in his former bodyguard despite himself.

At the sound of his voice, the Hyper beast's attention shifted. Its Hyper vines contracted with a sickening crunch and pulled the now-limp Enforcer into its abdomen. Satisfied with its catch, the beast's many spindly legs merged to form bulging muscles and tendons until it stood on six thick legs that raised it above the tallest building in the square. Its head was comprised of that hideous, snapping jaw filled with arm-length teeth, and its torso little more than an exposed ribcage holding both the Enforcer and Lees.

"Run!" Ike yelled. Meshi took off as fast as he could manage back toward the train.

The beast slammed to the ground, and its form shifted so fast Ike could have blinked and missed it. Hyper plates shifted with ear-shattering shrieks before this new shape launched itself at the retreating enemy. It quickly overtook him and slammed feet-first just ahead of him, cutting off Meshi's escape route.

Though wracked with a fear unlike any he'd ever felt, Meshi had to appreciate just how much detail the Hyper Object had put in transforming into something he feared. Its massive feline head rocked back and forth, faux beads of saliva falling to the ground from its exposed fangs. Even the crystalline surface was inscribed with lines to mimic patterned fur.

Meshi looked up at the crystalline purt, this snarling, fanged beast whose real-life counterpart would be just as happy ripping out his throat as lounging in a sunbeam. But this one was full of nothing but contempt for him. Bloodred stone barbs formed along its back, each ending in a wicked curve that could tear him apart in an instant.

He hadn't just failed his mission. He hadn't just lost to this mite. He was going to *die*.

So sure was Meshi of this belief that even after Ike slammed into his chest and hoisted him over his shoulder, even as he suffered the indignity of being carried like a child through the streets of this worthless town, he knew the beast would finish its task.

Meshi watched over Ike's shoulder as the beast shook itself violently before words finally emerged from its mouth, both in Lees' voice and not: "That's right. It's *your* turn to run."

Then, this Lees/Hyper beast screamed a metallic, unnatural roar against the fires raging around Last Light, and chased them with horrifying speed.

CHAPTER 16

The Hunt

Ike more or less ran blind through the smoke-filled alleys of the mining town. Ash coated his throat and sinuses, half-choking him as he struggled to hold Meshi over his shoulder. All he could really hear was the heavy sound of his own breathing, its wet rhythm interrupted at random intervals by distant explosions, followed by fresh peals of panicked shouting and aftershock tremors vibrating deep below.

Behind them, the Hyper beast was gaining ground. Even if he could see through the dense smoke, Ike couldn't risk a moment of distraction to glance over his shoulder to gauge how much trouble they were in.

The alley spilled them out onto the main thoroughfare. Their options were left or right, but Ike was turned around and couldn't find his bearings. Two people approached from the right and turned into the alley Ike and Meshi had just exited.

"Not that way! It's coming!" Ike managed to say through the smoke burning along his esophagus. His cough was a rattling rasp that forced him to double over. The pair looked up in horror, but Ike was already racing down the street to the left.

"*HRAAAAAAGH!*" The Hyper beast bellowed. Meshi twisted in Ike's arms, tipping him off balance and sending him careening into an older man running just ahead of them. The stranger took the brunt of Ike's weight and crumpled to the ground. Ike tripped over the man's splayed feet and caught himself, but not before Meshi tumbled from his perch and onto the ground.

"I'm sorry," Ike stammered. He reached to help the man up, trying to ignore Meshi's stifled cries of pain. The boy had thrown his gnarled hands out to catch himself and ripped open the wounds on his palms.

When Ike turned to lift Meshi again, the older man he'd just helped let out a strangled shout. The beast's heavy foot-falls were getting closer. Ike could see the shimmering red stone of its terrifying hide towering above the smoke now. The crystalline purt had grown nearly two stories in height during the pursuit.

"We gotta get you up, Meshi, come on now," Ike grunted

with the dead weight of his former client, travel companion, and – up until very recently – friend.

A sudden flash of red stopped him in his tracks. With supernatural speed, a dark figure appeared and darted down the main street, skidding to a halt near the alleyway. A shining thorn of golden Hyper erupted from their hand, and Ike barely recognized what they were holding. Smoke billowed around them as the force from the stake sent Hyper hurtling straight at the beast's skull.

Ike scrubbed at his face until his burning eyes refocused. Standing defiantly amidst the destruction, fire, and chaos, wielding Meshi's stolen stake with expert skill, was the proud proprietor of The Eye of Mite.

Ike smiled at witnessing the shaper's display of skill despite the terrifying situation. Jez's dark overcoat fluttered behind her where she stood her ground against an otherworldly beast six times her size.

The Hyper beast reared back in pain, noticing the second Hyper blast too late. It struggled to free itself from the yellow barb buried deep in its neck, connected by a thin strand to the stake in Jez's hand. She jerked it back, pulling the creature forward until its face was barely three feet above hers.

Jez's mouth was pressed into a determined line. She reeled the Hyper line back as she pulled, until it lay flat on its belly, its cries of frustration at an ear-splitting pitch. In one smooth move, Jez separated the strand from the weapon, lunged forward, and pointed it at the beast's heart.

"Wait, stop!" Ike sputtered. "Don't! It's Lees! Lees is inside!"

Jez looked over as if noticing him for the first time. She searched his face, saw his arm wrapped around Meshi, and then scowled.

"What did you do?"

"It's her! I swear it," Ike shouted.

It was just enough time for the beast to recover. One enormous claw pried the barb from its neck and crushed it. Then it howled and slammed its feet down in protest. Jez covered her ears and stumbled to the side to avoid a cascade of bricks breaking away from the nearby buildings. She looked at the beast, then back at Ike and Meshi, and swore loudly.

"Run!"

The three took off down the street away from the beast, Meshi once again bounding on Ike's shoulder. Now focused only on the person who hurt it, the beast ignored the older man and others on the streets to chase after the trio.

Since the angle of the sunlight pouring through this vision of Teeg's workshop hadn't shifted since the room formed, it was impossible to tell how much time had passed, but Lees' protesting shoulders and back gave the impression it had been hours.

Lees lounged back on a stool and fanned herself. Shaping

was far more taxing than she'd realized. Did everyone have this much trouble at first, or was this just another one of her failings as a mite?

"The whip is my favorite," She told the miniature Hyper. "But the claws and sword are pretty damn cool, too. Does it usually hurt this much?"

Miniature Hyper zoomed through the air and perched on her shoulder. It was warm and tickled where it touched her skin. Her many tiny aches and pains eased with the contact – still there, but only just.

"Thanks a lot," Lees said gratefully. The Hyper ball bounded around the room happily, then settled in front of her. "Oh, again? OK, let me think. Can it make me faster?"

As they ran through Last Light, Jez led them through the labyrinth of its tiers. She tried not to focus on the destruction around every corner, but the scenes of her home gnawed at her heart. Nearly every light post was knocked sideways, and many had toppled over completely. Those posts were surrounded by broken glass, the shattered Rapidite elements' glow receding. The group had to stop more than once to make way for families clutching bundles of valuables salvaged from their decimated apartments. Shop fronts that once held colorful, decorative signage now displayed little more than smoldering ashes. Deep fissures tore open the sidewalks and walkways, and the vines, shrubs, and Rapidite flowers the talented landshapers had managed to coax out of the hardened ground were withered to nothing. Most of the people they passed who weren't fleeing to higher ground with their loved ones were fighting to extinguish fires and clear rubble with their bare hands.

"Get out of here! It's not safe," Ike yelled over and over.

Some ignored them, some fled, and those who looked up at him and Jez caught the monstrous sight of the Hyper beast narrowing in on them. It was hot on their trails, seemingly accelerating with every step, oblivious to buildings and rails and anything else in its way in its pursuit.

"Spill. Is that the Hyper Object?" Jez asked, motioning for them to turn at an upcoming street and leading them to the top of a dizzying set of stairs.

"Yes. Isn't it magnificent?" Meshi replied. His gaze was fixed on the Hyper beast, his face a mix of awe and terror. Meshi bounced on Ike's shoulder as they hurried down the stairs, his mostly limp body flying up and back down with a thud.

"The damn stone consumed her. The Enforcer too," Ike said.

"It ate her!?" Jez exclaimed. Rage tinted her words, and Ike flinched.

"Not exactly. *She* ate *it*."

Jez stopped mid-step. Her wide eyes pierced through him, pinning him to the spot. He looked away, determined not to meet that gaze lest it stab right through him. Jez rolled her eyes and pulled his arm to keep them moving.

"Of all the stupid, idiotic moves," Jez hissed.

"I know... I don't know what she was thinking. She doesn't understand the stone's power."

"I was talking about you, you fucking useless prick!" Jez said. Ike flinched again. "You promised you would keep her safe. You weren't supposed to let something like this happen."

"I-I know, but she... I know. I'm sorry."

Jez looked straight ahead, and her vision blurred slightly. She passed the back of her hand over her eyes impatiently and sank her teeth into the side of her cheek. Now wasn't the time. She had to focus. Lees was in there. Lees was in danger.

"There's still a chance we can save her," Ike said with determination.

"What does that mean? You're saying there's a chance we *can't* save her!?" Jez stopped short at the bottom of the stairs. The beast paused at the top of the stairs and howled in anger or frustration or maybe a little of both. Ike stepped from the final stair and gingerly set Meshi down against a railing. Jez and Ike watched the beast warily, but it seemed stuck.

"The Hyper Object has taken over. She's part of it now," Meshi said breathlessly.

"Shut it, twerp. Ike, what're you talking about?" Jez snapped.

"I've seen it before," Ike started.

"Stop talking, Ike," Meshi warned.

"We've been studying it for a long time. The Hyper Object isn't like other Hyper, and Seers aren't like other shapers. You two, you can bend and move Hyper, but there's limits, and it doesn't cost you anything. With the Hyper Object, it's a give and take. What makes it so powerful is its ability to use a Seer's energy to make it stronger."

Ike paced as he spoke, raking one hand through his greying hair. The ring of the crown on his finger winked in and out of view. Jez watched him with narrowed eyes.

"Seers can push it past its breaking point, but the same goes for the Hyper Object. That stone can absorb the Seer's energy and stamina beyond their limits. If it keeps this up – if she doesn't break free –" He avoided looking at Jez as he faltered.

"It'll be fused like *that* forever," Meshi blurted out, unable to keep himself from interrupting Ike any longer. He balanced on the railing with his elbows while gently wrapping his shredded hands, wincing as he did. Meshi focused on this work as he continued, sighing loud enough for everyone to hear him, "The longer she's in beast mode like this, the faster the Hyper Object consumes her. It's not just physical either. It's wrapped around her brain, too, blinding her with visions of its power and potential. She's doomed."

"She'll die?" Jez asked sharply. Ike grimaced. "That thing will suck her dry and seal her inside?"

"Oh yes, without a doubt," Meshi said flippantly. "If only *I* had the stone, this –

Jez reached forward without missing a beat and pulled him off the railing by his collar.

"I asked you politely to *shut up* once, but I guess it takes a little more to get through that thick skull," She said. Meshi raised an eyebrow at Ike.

"There's no need for all that," Ike said quickly. Jez glared at him but didn't put Meshi down. Ike tried again. "All hope isn't lost, Meshi, so stop saying it is. Lees is strong enough to fight against it. We just need to give her a little help."

"Separating its head from the body would help," Meshi suggested. Jez growled and pressed her forearm against his windpipe. A strangled sound escaped his throat.

"You won't lay a finger on Lees. Suggest it again, and your face is gonna match those hands," She threatened. Meshi nodded furiously. Jez reluctantly dropped him and turned to Ike.

"If we could pin the beast down, we might be able to pull Lees out," Ike suggested. "We need to find a way to – wait. Where did it go?"

Jez whipped around to look up the stairs, and Meshi squealed in surprise. A crystalline tendril darted between their legs and twisted around Meshi's arm. Ike wrapped his arms around the tendril and squeezed, giving Meshi just enough wiggle room to pull his arm free.

A winding path of destruction through balconies, barriers, and fences marked the beast's path down to their tier. Stairs were too much for its many legs, but barreling through solid stone and concrete was apparently child's play. Jez had to admire its strength.

Not to be stopped, the Hyper beast reached out its many arms, the number multiplying as it did, aiming solely for Meshi. Ike rolled Meshi over himself to avoid being crushed, then hauled him to his feet. Jez watched the Hyper beast's focus stay on Meshi. It hadn't been after her, despite Jez shooting it with Hyper. It was after him.

"Give it what it wants!" She said suddenly. "It's after him. Hand over the kid, and it'll be distracted enough for us to pin it down. I still have the stake."

"I'm right here, you know!" Meshi said indignantly.

"Let it kill him? I can't do that," Ike said. He shielded Meshi from another whip-like tentacle, which sliced his forearm from wrist to elbow. Ike groaned and pulled Meshi further away.

"Whose side are you on?" Jez asked.

"Not about sides. It's...*ow! Meshi, move!*... It's complicated!" Ike said.

The beast was getting closer. Its many scuttling, razor-sharp legs tore apart cobblestone and metal railings with ease. They were running out of areas that hadn't felt the brunt of the squire's explosive assaults. Sharp barbs of red Hyper sank into the ground around them, mimicking the one from the Hyper stake that Jez shot at the beast before she knew it was Lees. Apparently, her actions had struck a nerve.

"DOWN!" Jez nimbly hopped over a Hyper pillar in her

path and hooked an arm around a railing, letting her momentum swing her onto the stairs leading down to the next tier. Ike quickly followed with Meshi in tow. As he caught up to her, Jez took a deep breath to bellow, "You gotta step up and make a choice, Ike!"

"Can one of you two idiots do something before I'm eaten, too?" Meshi yelled. Jez reached over to smack him on the side of his bobbing head. Ike swatted her away before she could hit him again and pointed ahead.

"We could lose it through the fires," He shouted.

"Too many people are trying to put them out. We'll be leading it right to them," Jez argued as they continued further away from the beast.

"Jez?" A weak voice called out through the smoke.

It was Midge, sitting with a group of people huddled in the entryway of a municipal building. Several lay prone on the ground with others tending to their wounds. All of them still wore their dusty orange mining uniforms.

Jez stopped to inspect Midge's shoulder. A deep laceration oozed blood, but someone had taped the skin together to staunch the flow. Meshi slid from Ike's shoulder and curled his lip at the injury before turning away. Midge pointed a shaky finger to the other side of the street, where a high fence separated them from the drop to the next tier down.

A streak of smoke arced from below them, and something exploded.

"It's one of those squires," The woman tending to Midge

whispered. "She's hollarin' and settin' off explosives left and right. No idea what she's using."

"THIS IS OUR TOWN NOW!" A reedy voice practically cackled from below. The woman furrowed her brow and shook her head.

"She's the one settin' all them fires. When people runnin' out of houses, she's shootin' at them."

Ike reached down to help the now-bandaged Midge lean back, but she waved him off.

"A kid," Midge wheezed. She coughed and tried again, "Crazy lady grabbed a kid. Dunno why. Think it was Morrigan, but hard to tell. Nailed me with that stake of hers before I could get 'em back."

"They have stakes?" Meshi asked quickly. Jez studied his face, could practically see the wheels turning, but she pushed it from her mind. The biggest danger wasn't below them.

"You all need to move. There's something coming, and if you don't get out of the way you'll be crushed by it," Jez warned. "I'll square up with the squire. You stay and help the others."

Meshi tapped Ike's shoulder and pointed behind him. "Ike, I can help! They've got a kid, right? I can go find them. And, um, help keep them safe."

"Hold on a second," Ike said, but Meshi was already hustling to catch up with Jez.

"You stay there and help out. I'll be back!" He called over his shoulder.

Despite the limping and sniveling Meshi had been overcome with just moments ago, he effortlessly kept in lockstep with Jez as she vaulted over the safety railing and scampered down the wall.

Unlike the other, this lone squire had kept her helmet on, though one of the golden cheek guards had been ripped away, and the visor was dented. A bandolier hung awkwardly across her chest with half its ammunition missing. Half the structures near the street were carved out and caved in, handiwork of this deranged squire and the other half of the grenades. A stake swung from the holster on her hip. Beneath one leather-clad arm, frozen in terror, hung a young girl with long blond hair.

"Oho! They're sending more brave souls in to stop me, eh?" The squire squealed when Jez and Meshi approached.

"Go grab the girl," Jez barked at him.

"Me? Absolutely not. I'm not getting close to crazy over there," Meshi scoffed.

Jez walked slowly toward the squire, who ripped at her bandolier with her free hand and slipped a small grenade free. Jez recognized it as a slightly more advanced version of what the excavation crew used to widen drifts or open chambers. She froze and slowly put her hands up, palms facing the squire.

"She's just a kid. You don't want her blood on your hands."

"You think I care about some earthworm blood?" The

squire threw her head back and laughed. "You forget that you moles serve us. That's your only purpose. We use you for target practice, you dig up our Hyper, you keep us happy and fed. Whatever happens to you isn't really your choice."

Jez inched closer. The squire held the grenade to her face, pulled the pin out with her teeth, and lobbed it over her head. Meshi scampered out of the way before it exploded. Pieces of shrapnel and rock hit Jez's back, and pinpricks of pain scuttled along the backs of her arms. She flinched but kept inching forward.

CRACK! Lees swore as her forehead connected with the wall near the back door. Her conjured, Hyper-bulked body with half-formed wings deflated as stars swam across her vision.

"It's impossible to keep control when you're that big!" She whined. "Like trying to drive a Granby cart down the tier stairways. I'm *never* doing that again."

The Hyper ball touched itself to her forehead, and the angry throbbing ebbed away. But there was something lurking beneath that pain that wasn't going away. A thought she couldn't quite grasp was gnawing at her. She'd forgotten to do something, or was supposed to be doing something, or what was it?

"This has been helpful and all, but I need to get out of here," Lees said.

Cramps gripped her stomach, hitting her so suddenly she doubled over. The Hyper ball flitted erratically between the windows and the superheated door. It paused its pacing to touch her, but the pain in her gut was unchanged. Voices shouted just beyond that door, voices she might know or should know, but there was something blocking the connection between sound and recognition.

"Is someone in trouble?" Lees asked through gritted teeth.

The Hyper ball suddenly burst into a hundred tendrils that each whipped around just as frantically before being sucked back into its ball form. It repeated this again. Lees held out a hand without thinking, fighting against the force of the cramps, and blood-red spears sprouted from her nailbeds.

"Think you're a tough one, huh?" The squire unholstered the deadly stake and pressed it against the young girl's cheek. "Go ahead. I'm dying to see what this does at close range."

Jez diverted her attention behind the squire for a moment, then locked eyes with the young girl.

"Close your eyes," She whispered.

A sprinting figure collided with the squire. He came from the side while the squire was distracted, catching her in the faceplate's blind spot. Jez ran the last few feet and secured her arms around the child. As Teeg wrestled the squire to the ground, Jez hurried the girl toward the stairs leading back up to the higher tier.

Meshi shifted from one foot to the other, not moving to help but instead staring down at the ground with great interest.

The squire shoved Teeg off and wriggled to her feet, panting hard and grumbling in the heavy armor. He scrambled to his feet and squared up, keeping his arms raised to protect his face. But no stance would protect him against the squire's arsenal. Helmet knocked askew, face pulled into a crazed smile, the squire pointed her weapon at Teeg's heart and held another grenade aloft – its pin separated and flung to the side.

"I decide when you die," She sneered. Her hand pressed tighter around the stake's handle, and a tiny flash of light ignited the mechanism that would fire the Hyper bolt with its deadly-fast trajectory right into Teeg's chest.

Jez was too far away. Meshi was unable or unwilling to intervene. Teeg steeled himself for an attack from which he'd never get up.

Tears welled up in Jez's eyes. She'd kill the squire for this, tear her limb from limb, leave nothing for them to return to her family. Jez blinked to clear her eyes, and something landed at her feet.

The severed crystal tentacle wiggled ineffectually on the ground, one end still sizzling from the heat and force of catching the bolt.

Another monstrous tendril slid into view before coiling around the squire and lifting her into the air like a puppet. The grenade rolled back into the fog, and the stake flew in an arc to land somewhere near Meshi and Jez.

Teeg's hands searched his chest and, finding himself quite alive and whole, dropped to his knees. He stared at the gnarled stump of the tentacle that had saved his life and watched the oozing red innards pool on the ground. An electrifying power radiated from the puddle. Teeg felt it deep in his veins, ten times more powerful than any Hyper he'd ever encountered. More out of curiosity than anything else, he raised a hand and tried to pull on the Hyper the way he'd seen shapers move. Tiny droplets responded by bubbling along the pool's surface for a second or two before the entire tentacle, puddle and all, was sucked backward.

His eyes followed its path up and up and up until his eyes landed on... his mind kicked and screamed against the image, and the only word he could conjure to describe what he was seeing was *nightmare*. The beast stood high enough to tower over the tops of this tier's buildings. It was a mass of tentacles the width of the mine shaft with swirling red Hyper roiling beneath a transparent skin. Rows of teeth lined an impossibly wide mouth, above which the squire, fighting valiantly but pointlessly, dangled.

Something touched the small of his back, and Teeg's heart nearly gave out as he whipped around. It was only Jez who had finally made it back to where he stood. Her fingers dug into Meshi's arm, who looked suspiciously compliant.

"Shit, she got big!" Someone called out. Teeg looked past Jez to see Ike running toward them, his tan cloak whipping behind him.

"What the hell is that thing?" Teeg demanded. Jez moved her hand up to his shoulder.

"Your daughter," Meshi snapped as Ike reached the group now. Teeg's face drained of color. He looked to Jez in desperation for an explanation.

"It's the Hyper Object," Jez said quickly. "It overtook Lees, but we're going to save her." She jerked her arm back to pull Meshi closer, "And we're gonna do it by giving this brat to that thing."

"Hey!" Meshi and Ike interjected at once.

"It wants to eat you, so we let it, and while it's distracted, we pry Lees free." She stared directly at Ike as she finished.

"She's trapped in there?" Teeg asked.

"Keep up, old man," Meshi snorted. He clawed at Jez's hand to try to free himself, but she was much stronger than him. He shifted gears, pleading, "It doesn't have to be me. Please, don't do this. It's going after all those idiots wrecking this stupid town, use them for a distraction."

Somehow, the Hyper beast managed to open its mouth even wider than before. The squire struggled weakly as she stared down at the toothy void in horror, and Jez looked away right as the tentacle loosened its grip.

Chapter 16

"Teeg," Jez said suddenly. "Go get Jeri. Find Ekoli and her son, what's-his-name. We need all the shapers we have. Bring everyone back to the train station."

Teeg nodded and left without another word.

"What're you thinking?" Ike asked.

Jez stared at the Hyper beast's chest, where its heart should be, and though it couldn't have been possible through the layers of its Hyper armor, she could have sworn she saw Lees just inside, nervously flattening her hair and giving her a sideways smile that made her stomach flutter. This image of Lees wasn't trapped in a suffocating coffin draining her life away. No, she was perched on a barstool at the Eye of Mite. Her cheeks lightly flushed after finishing a pint – she's always been a light weight, her Lees – and her eyes searching for her across the bar when she thought Jez wasn't looking.

She kept her focus on this vision, half invention and half memory, and slowly removed the golden rings from her fingers. Each one unraveled and melted into the next until she had a long coil of Hyper that suddenly glowed a soft yellow.

"We're going to save Lees, even if we have to pull that beast apart bit by bit to do it."

CHAPTER 17

The Final Push

Smoke lingered at the edges of the Last Light train station, which had been nearly destroyed during the fight with the overzealous Enforcer. The block housing for the town-wide zipline cable system at one end of the trainyard was untouched, though two of the cables hung unusually low. The train still sat at the station, motionless and empty, mercifully undamaged, but the same wasn't true for the rest of the area. Craters marred the cobblestone walkways that were now covered in concrete dust and debris. Piles of crumbled bricks were scattered around nearby buildings that had sustained significant damage, revealing dollhouse-like scenes of living rooms and stairwells behind the ruined walls. Half of the stairs leading up to the train platform were obliterated.

Crimson streaks, half hidden beneath the wreckage of the station, were all that remained of the day's bloody struggle.

Those who had witnessed the fight between Lees and the Enforcer were nowhere to be seen. Most had rushed off to help put out fires and escape the beast's path of destruction. In their absence, the trainyard was eerily quiet as two pairs of footsteps rushed to the scene from an adjoining street to the north.

Ike reached the center of the courtyard first, followed by a wheezing, swearing Meshi. Despite the careful binding Ike had wrapped around his hands before they left the lower tier, blood still dripped from Meshi's fingertips and streaked his forearms. Ike slowed to a stop. Meshi, whose worried gaze was focused behind him, collided with Ike.

"Damnit, watch where you're going!" Meshi snapped. Reluctant to rely on his injured hands, he awkwardly shuffled on the ground and rolled sideways to scramble back up. "Hey! Are you even listening to me?"

"They're not here," Ike replied. It took Ike's eyes a moment to adjust to the courtyard's darkness. Smoke all but blacked out any street lamp that hadn't been broken during the explosions, so the area was lit solely by the overhead Rapidite's anemic yellow glow.

"What do you mean? This is the spot, isn't it? That vile woman–" Meshi sputtered.

"Jez," Ike interrupted.

"She said to lure it here, right? She-she tricked us! She

told us to come here to make it easier for that thing to eat us!" Meshi's voice rose in panic. "I should have known better than to trust these low-life degenerates! They're snakes, liars, two-timing worms who – *GAAAAH!*"

The Hyper beast schlorped out into the courtyard mouth first with a nauseating, gut-wrenching splat. Free from the confines of the alleyway, its amorphous, jelly-like form collapsed into a wide puddle. Meshi and Ike could do little else but stand amidst the destruction of the earlier fight and watch the beast writhe on the ground until it regained its composure. Jagged edges of crystalized Hyper bubbled from the center, clumping together until an angular monster emerged, still easily two stories tall, sporting just two thick arms and equally sturdy, tree-trunk legs. Its purt-like head reemerged, snarling mouth bursting with foot-long incisors.

One step, then two – each footfall of the newly-formed Hyper beast rattled Ike's teeth. Try as he might, it was impossible to see it as anything other than a mindless monster. He stepped protectively in front of Meshi, aware that the beast's eyes remained fixed on the boy alone.

But this is where Jez told them to be.

"St-stay back!" Meshi screeched hoarscly at the beast. "Hey! HEY! Anytime would be great, you idiots!" He scanned the trainyard again. Still nothing. "We could really use some help now, damnit!"

At the sound of his voice, the beast reared back and roared in response. Meshi cowered behind Ike but continued yelling, even louder than before, cursing Jez and begging for her help in the same breath.

A low hum filled the air, followed by mechanical whirring and a persistent beeping. The many crisscrossed zipline cables high above them slowly shifted down the sturdy support beams, each nearly tall enough to touch the cavern ceiling. Ike couldn't help but marvel at the intricacies of the system in motion – each cable could move independently to bring goods or people from any one tier to another.

Then the beast landed back on all fours, shaking the ground and jolting Ike back to their very immediate danger. Those cables were moving far too slowly. The beast's glossy eyes narrowed. Its crystalline ears twitched. It sauntered toward them with the gait of a predator stalking its cornered prey, taking its time. Ike braced himself.

Snarling, the Hyper beast's paws left the ground as it lunged to clear Ike and devour its prey. Meshi whimpered and curled into a ball, but the attack never came. The beast gave a choked yelp – one of the descending cables caught it mid-pounce and slammed the creature to the ground. Meshi opened one eye to see the beast tangled on the ground. He snorted and sneered at it until the beast let out another bone-shaking roar that sent him reeling back.

The Hyper beast wasn't done yet. It crawled out from under the cable and crouched low, preparing to pounce once more. Then a strand of shimmering gold looped around its neck and cinched tightly.

"Good work," Jez appeared briefly between the beast's arms and waved at Ike. Winding the yellow Hyper rope around her arm, she pulled the strand tight to lift her off the ground. Ike watched open-mouthed as she used the Hyper like a climbing rope, kicking off the beast's bicep and shoulder for leverage until she could shimmy into place on its back.

The beast's arms weren't jointed correctly to reach its back, so its only option was to arch its back and thrash to remove this new, annoying threat. Jez whooped, then she dug in her knees and lifted her butt, rolling with the beast while it tried desperately to buck her off. "C'mon, people, let's go!"

Others emerged from around the courtyard so quickly that Ike jumped in surprise. They'd been waiting for her signal, exactly like she'd told him they would.

More zipline cables descended along their tracks, adding to the cacophony of mechanical whirring and beeping alarms now echoing from every direction. Though all zipline cables are connected at one end to the housing block at the train station, their other ends run to housing blocks scattered throughout the town, forming a crisscrossed grid that connects all of Last Light.

An older woman wearing a baker's apron and a patchwork shirt rushed forward. She pulled a handful of tiny blue pebbles from her pocket, cocked her arm back, and lobbed them at the beast's head. Each hit their target and exploded on impact, emitting flashes of blue light so bright their afterimage seared Ike's eyes even from where he stood. The beast's pupils shrank until they nearly disappeared in the inky whiteness of its irises, and it roared in pain at the pebble shards embedded in its crystal shell.

"Under the zipline, Ekoli!" Jez called. The baker nodded and jogged to the left, throwing another salvo of industrial crackle shards that forced the beast to stumble sideways to avoid them.

Eria directed his crew on either end of the first zipline cable to reach the ground. Jez separated a Hyper strand from the beast's reins and looped it below them. With the crew's help, Jez and Eria lifted the enormous cable off the ground. Ekoli launched another handful of exploding shards at its back legs, knocking it off balance in its scramble to avoid the attack. The ground shook as the beast fell prone.

"Now!" Jez shouted. Eria's crew threw the zipline cable over one of the beast's outstretched legs. Two ran to the nearest housing block to manually tighten it, signaling to the others stationed blocks away to do the same. The beast twisted against the trap, but its leg held fast. Jez teetered dangerously on its back and slipped, scrambling to grasp the Hyper rope in time to swing down in front of its snapping jaws and land safely in a heap near Ike.

Ekoli rounded the beast from behind to reach Jez, but its tail swung around and dug into her stomach, knocking her to the ground. Crackle shards flew from her pocket and skittered around her. She didn't have time to squeeze her eyes shut before they exploded in blinding flashes of blue light.

"Ma!" A gangly kid who couldn't have been much older than 12 stumbled forward. Ekoli let him help her up, but pushed him away from the beast. She rubbed her eyes vigorously. The boy frowned and opened his fist to reveal a flattened rectangle of yellow Hyper, about the size of a pencil. He held it with his fingertips and pulled, his mouth pressed tight with effort as he expanded it by barely an inch.

A second cable reached the ground. Eria and his crew hustled to repeat the snare as two more cables descended, falling perpendicular to the beast's back. Jez tucked in her arms and rolled away from the beast, stopping to grunt in Ike's direction, "Eria needs a minute with those cables – keep it distracted!"

Ike looked hesitantly at Meshi, who flared his nostrils and rolled his eyes before shouting, "Eat shit, you stupid Hyper beast!"

Immediately, the beast ceased its flailing against the cable holding it down and snarled in Meshi's direction. The boy quickly ducked behind Ike again.

Jez swung the Hyper lasso above her head and sent it sailing through the air. It ensnared the beast's right arm at the same time the two descending cables pressed against its back. The cracked stone facade crumbled from the already damaged buildings with the force of the beast's fall. Eria cackled and shouted, "That's for always bein' a pain in the ass, Lees!"

More cables descended overhead, the high-pitched

grinding of metal on metal growing louder and louder as they announced their slow arrival.

Ekoli stumbled over to Jez, who held out an arm to stabilize the woman still reeling from the close-range explosions. She watched the beast thrash, snarling and testing the cables' strength. But Eria's men knew what they were doing.

Then the beast stopped moving entirely. The crew in the courtyard watched warily as the beast's skin bubbled with a sickening gurgle. Thick, mucus-like Hyper oozed from its pores and pooled around the cables across its back and leg. Once all three were fully encased, the Hyper hardened into the same shining crystalline substance of the rest of its body.

Jez held her breath.

Pop! Pop! Individual strands of the thick, twisted cables groaned and snapped under the pressure of the hardened Hyper.

"Ah, shit. Where the hell is Teeg?" Jez shouted. She caught three people in Eria's crew backing away from the beast, appearing moments from running away, and pointed at them. "Hey! You! Go find him!"

Meshi leaned forward to whisper into Ike's ear. When the bodyguard looked back in surprise, Meshi nodded his head toward the beast and raised his eyebrows. Ike waved the boy off and hissed something back.

Every few seconds, another *pop!* signaled the cables' weakening, and the beast bided its time by eying them all with fury and flexing against the bindings holding it in place.

"Sorry there, Jez! *This one* was takin' a nap." Teeg hustled into the courtyard opposite the beast, holding Jeri's arm in a death grip. He paused when he caught sight of the beast, then dragged Jeri forward. When they reached Jez, Jeri pulled his arm free and stretched it leisurely.

"Didn't realize snoozing on the job was a crime, boss," Jeri grumbled, not bothering to stifle a yawn. "Don't know what you want me to do about all this."

The crew members Jez had sent away practically sprinted into the courtyard. They shuffled back into the group, looking down or away from where they'd come. Seconds later, four green-uniformed figures limped into the courtyard. Teeg started toward them in alarm, but they weren't injured. They carefully carried the incapacitated and bound body of the squire who had started the fire in the mine. When they reached the stairway to the train platform, they unceremoniously dumped him to the ground.

"Very good, very good. We'll ship him back with the others once we round them up," Town Chief Marshall told his chippers happily. "That should send a message to anyone thinking about – well, well. What's all this?"

Marshall thrust his hands behind his back and straightened his back. He surveyed the courtyard, taking in the overridden zipline cable system, the struggling Hyper beast, and the townspeople frozen in confusion. When he spotted Jez, his eyes lit up.

"My dear, what is going on?"

Jez stifled a smile at the thought of Lees, who would be gagging and rolling her eyes at the pet name. The beast roared behind her, and a pit formed back in her stomach. She swallowed hard.

"Nice. They can deal with all that. I'm going back," Jeri announced. Teeg snatched him by the front of his shirt before he could turn.

"We sure could use your help," Jez said breathlessly. Marshall tilted his head to take another look at the beast and gave a half-hearted shrug.

"This isn't really what we do..." He said.

"Useless chippers! Whaddya do for us 'cept overwork us? Care more about that mine than any of us!" Eria shouted. The uniformed chippers who had brought in the squire looked to their leader, though one of them brushed his hand across his hip and glared at Eria.

"But —" Jez began to say.

CRRRACK! One of the two cables across the beast's back snapped. Hyper tendrils flung the two pieces away from it.

Town Chief Marshall startled, then cleared his throat. "This uh... Well, this sorta thing falls outside our jurisdiction." He stared past Jez in awe of the giant beast struggling to break free. "Looks like there's nothing we can do here."

He waved at his men to follow him. After three measured steps out of the courtyard, he picked up the pace to run far away from the train station. "That thing gets into the mine, that's a different story!" He yelled back toward the crowd.

"Buncha cowards!" Eria screamed after them.

CRRRRACK! The cable around the beast's leg snapped.

"Jeri! Help them!" Teeg growled.

"And do what?" Jeri waved his hands around. "You think I'm some kind of beast wrangler? What could I – is that Bertrax?"

Teeg followed Jeri's finger to where Ekoli's son stood, still furiously trying to pull apart the Hyper in his hands. His lip quivered as his motions became more erratic, blushing furiously as he failed to expand it more than another few centimeters.

Jeri sighed so deeply that Teeg was surprised his chest didn't collapse. "Hey, kid, c'mere. Watch this." Jeri turned to Jez and said, "I'll help, but I want tomorrow off."

He walked closer to the beast and looked up to survey the zipline cables still descending. He reached into his breast pocket and flung what looked like yellow confetti into the air.

CRRRRACK! The final cable holding the beast down snapped.

"Anytime now, Jeri," Jez warned. The beast extended its claws and swiped at Ekoli, then at Eria, shaking its head back and forth as if looking for something.

"Can't rush art," Jeri said snidely to Bertrax, who had cautiously approached the ornery cook.

The minuscule pieces of Hyper that Jeri had thrown landed together along the cable immediately above them, then broke into smaller groups that leapt higher and higher to reach the other cables, until the entire zipline system was glittering with yellow Hyper. Each piece wriggled between the tightly wound fibers of the cables and, now unseen, raced to the pulley systems at each end.

Jeri reached his arms high above his head. With a wink at Bertrax, he closed his fists and brought them down, pulling himself into a deep squat.

Loud enough to wake the dead, the puttering motors in the block housing squealed with the force of every cable simultaneously slamming to the ground. The townspeople gathered there jumped in all directions to avoid being crushed by the tangled grid.

Bertrax's eyes widened. This close, he could see that Jeri hadn't tossed Hyper dust in the air but was manipulating dozens of thin, nearly invisible strings made of yellow Hyper. Every string was woven around his fingers and covered his wrists, flexing and relaxing as Jeri twisted and danced to operate the zipline machinery. The baker's son watched in awe, not meaning to clench his fist so hard around his own Hyper. Something sharp and warm wriggled against his palm.

Jez's ears were left ringing from the beast's desperate roar and Jeri's actions. She pushed her fingers into her ears to lessen the auditory assault. Jeri leaned to the right, then to the left from that squatting position. He flexed his ankles to push himself back and forth, twisting the cables around the beast's form until it was tightly pinned.

Teeg rushed forward as soon as it was clear the beast

wasn't going anywhere. Jeri stopped Bertrax from following and held out his hand to take the piece of Hyper he was trying to manipulate. Jeri waved his hand through the air in a flowing motion, pulling the sheet of Hyper into a plate half his height before shrinking it back down to pencil size. He tapped his chest, then repeated the motion. The boy nodded so vigorously that Ike thought his neck might snap in half.

"Next part's tricky, fellas," Teeg said. He and Jez were just out of range of the beast's snapping jaws. "We gotta pry those damn jaws open an' keep 'em that way. Lees is in there, and we're gonna pull her out."

Eria scoffed loudly and nudged another of the miners standing next to him. Jez shot Eria a scathing look, and he jerked his head down, ears turning pink.

Jez threaded a Hyper strand around one of the cables right in front of the beast's face.

"Quickly! Get its mouth open!" Teeg snapped. The assembled group pushed the cable against the beast's mouth, but they weren't strong enough to pry it apart. Jez quickly separated another strand of her Hyper and used it to slap the beast's snout. It snapped its jaws at the attack instinctively, allowing the group to push the cable fully between those glistening, razor-sharp teeth. The beast crunched down on the makeshift bit, but the zipline cable was made of stronger stuff. Thick globs of Hyper oozed from its gums to encase the cable that was forcing its mouth open.

"If any of you drops those cables or lets it free, you're cut off from the booze forever," Jez threatened, pointing a stern finger at the crowd.

"Don't even joke about that..." Someone mumbled.

Out of the corner of her eye, Jez caught Meshi yelling at Ike, who was trying to put his hands on the boy's shoulders to calm him down. After a short interaction, Ike moved to the front line to help keep the beast stable. He stepped up next to Jez and Teeg, planted his feet in the bottom half of the beast's jaw, and shoved his entire weight against it. He nodded curtly, and Jez returned it.

"Let's go get our girl."

Teeg and Jez pressed their torsos into the beast's mouth and throat, crawling out of sight. The moment they reached down the giant's gullet, all hell broke loose. As if tapping into a new reserve of furious energy, the beast fought with renewed strength against its bonds. Tendrils sprang out from its back to swing wildly and blindly at its captors.

Ekoli juked the tendril closest to her with the agility of a boxer, then bodyslammed it to the ground. Its end fluttered uselessly against her weight. Ekoli rested on her forearms and crushed the tendril between her thighs, shouting, "Like that!"

"Yaaaaaaah!" Eria's screech echoed in surround sound clarity as one particularly nasty tendril hoisted him by the waist and whipped him side to side. "I'll never forgive her for this *aaaaah!*"

More of the townspeople were rejoining them in the square, having put out the fires that were still burning and realizing the squires had ceased their path of destruction. Those who weren't frozen in fear at the sight of the Hyper beast sprang into action to help hold down cables and ropes and tackle rogue tendrils.

Someone knocked down a tendril with a pile driver so expertly executed that Jez would have been impressed had she seen it. Two teens who usually worked on excavation crews swung their pickaxes at another tendril, stabbing it through the hardened exterior and pinning it down.

Bertrax was hard at work following Jeri's instructions. His unofficial teacher jumped up and down in genuine excite-ment, watching the young shaper manipulate the Hyper into a thin sheet the size of his head. A red Hyper tendril jabbed into his side, and on instinct, he slammed the sheet down on it, neatly slicing it in half. Jeri grabbed the boy and lifted him into the air, dancing around the severed tendril wriggling independently on the ground.

Away from the flurry of activity outside, Teeg and Jez had reached the heart of the beast – or at least where the heart would be. There was the Enforcer, curled into a fetal position, clutching his wound that had stopped bleeding for now. He was shaking softly, clearly alive but unaware of their pres-ence. And then the squire, whose midsection was partially caved in, as if a giant fist had crushed her. Jez looked away before she could assess whether they were still breathing.

Tremors shook the beast. Teeg and Jez braced themselves as best they could.

Finally, there she was. *Lees*. All four limbs stretched out and encased in jagged, twisting Hyper. Her eyes were closed, face contorted in pained confusion. Jez rushed out to place a hand on Lees' face. Before her skin could connect with hers, a layer of Hyper slithered over Lees' cheek. It was ice-cold and bit at Jez's fingers. Her skin stuck to its surface before she was able to yank it back.

"Lees, kiddo, please, you gotta wake up," Teeg sputtered. He pushed as close as possible without actually touching her. "We're here now, you're not alone. Hey. Come on, Lees. Just give us a sign you can hear me."

Lees stayed on the floor of Teeg's workshop until the beams on the ceiling came back into focus. Sharp, stabbing pain still radiated through her guts, but it was more manageable now that she'd figured out how to retract those spears from her fingers. The miniature Hyper ball flitted anxiously above her, occasionally resting on her chest before shooting back up into the air.

"Lees, c'mon, can you hear me?"

The world spun again when she shot up from the ground. Muffled voices were on the other side of that superheated door, just outside the workshop. She held onto the counters for balance and stumbled over to strain her ears.

"Is that Teeg? Jez? What's going on, are they…? Hey! Hey, Teeg! Jez! You there!?"

Miniature Hyper pressed into her chest, pushing her away from the dangerously hot door. Lees gently shoved it aside and leaned in again.

"We came to get you out! Is there anything you can do to help?"

Flames licked away from the doorframe, grazing her chest. She pulled back and glared at the miniature Hyper.

"What do they mean, help? Get me out of where?"

Lees studied the door, then narrowed her focus to the erratic Hyper in front of her. "Let me through that door."

Visions pressed in from both sides, sending an icepick through both temples as images of Teeg relaxing in her room flooded her mind. Except none of her stuff was there. Instead of a bed and dresser, there was an overstuffed armchair and a beautiful wooden bar cart. He poured himself a glass of amber-colored liquid and sighed contentedly. Then she saw Jez wiping down the counters at The Eye of Mite, flirting brazenly with a beautiful brunette woman whose fingertips grazed Jez's arm, her head thrown back in laughter.

"Are you kidding me? That's not – you're just fishing now. Come on, that's enough. You've shown me how to use you, so let me through that door."

An unmarked grave – *hers*. That beautiful stranger fixing The Great Mechanized BurgerMaker 5000 while Jez watched admiringly – *Lees scoffed at that one* – and then a surge of frustration bubbled up in her chest that was not her own.

Then her mother, a nasty grin on her face that she'd never seen before, secretly passing money to the chippers who ripped her from her life. Cackling to herself back home after Lees was dragged onto the train.

"That's enough!" Lees snapped. She mentally pressed against the images, wresting control for the moment. The miniature Hyper dipped lower in response.

"*I'm* the one in control here. Not you. It doesn't work like that. If I'm a Seer, then I'm a shaper. You're the Hyper. That's how this is going to be."

Lees blocked out all other distractions, even the voices behind the door. She could feel the Hyper Object pushing against her mental resolve, trying to blind her with more images of whatever horrible thing it could conjure. *But it wasn't real.*

She repeated this a few times, a new mantra to force that image of her mother out of her head.

"If you want to be partners, then you need to let me go."

Flames darted beneath the doorframe, but the heat was already subsiding. Lees tentatively touched a knuckle to the doorknob, and it was cool once more. She let out the breath she'd been holding and nodded before opening it.

Almost imperceptibly, one of the thorny vines connecting Lees' arm to the ceiling retreated.

"There you go," Teeg said soothingly. "Come back to us now. That's it."

The Hyper holding her left foot shrank slowly. Another released its vice grip on her right knee. Teeg gingerly wrapped an arm around Lees' waist so she wouldn't fall if – *no, when* – she was finally freed. Tiny pieces of Hyper jabbed at him as he grabbed her, but the pinpricks were nothing compared to what she must be feeling, so he did his best to ignore them.

"That's it, you're doing great. You've got this under control. We're here, me and Jez, we got you," Teeg continued.

Her eyes remained closed, but the lines of Lees' face eased. The final piece of Hyper holding her right hand liquefied and oozed down her elbow, armpit, hip, then slipped past her leg onto the ground. But her arm didn't flop down. She reached out a shaking hand to grasp Teeg's shoulder. Every finger twitched erratically, but her grip was firm.

Jez put her hand on Lees' free side to help Teeg hold her up. She kept her eyes focused on Lees' face, ignoring the Enforcer's guttural groaning as he regained consciousness.

Lees' lips moved, but she made no sound. Teeg pressed his ear near her lips, trying to catch whatever she was mouthing. Jez held her breath, desperately willing Lees to open her eyes, say something, move, anything.

"Come on, Lees, it's time. Open your eyes. We gotta get you out of here," Teeg whispered.

All else was quiet. The beast stopped fighting against its bonds, and the townspeople dutifully kept its jaws pried open. Something like a whimper escaped Lees' mouth. Only her left arm remained woven into the fabric of the beast, and even that was easing bit by bit, retreating upward or melting down her body to be reabsorbed.

Teeg fully wrapped his arms around Lees' torso and nodded to Jez. The last of the Hyper holding her in place liquefied and pooled on her chest, seeming completely inert.

Carefully, they pulled Lees through the beast's throat and into its mouth, the beast's jaws hanging in a fang-lined opening to safety. Ike stood just outside, his arms down, ready to pull them up.

People surrounding the beast cheered at Teeg and Jez's successful rescue mission. Yells and cries of joy erupted from the crowd, interrupted by someone's frantic movement. Meshi pushed his way through the crowd of people now. "Out of my way! Move! Get away from me!" He yelled and glared at the trio emerging from the beast's jaws.

Jez appeared first. Then Teeg, followed by Lees' slow, staggered movements. Teeg held one of her arms to guide her through the opening.

Meshi watched Lees' hand emerge, stretching up toward the Rapidite above them. His blood boiled at the sight – and at Ike's eagerness to be on scene and associated with this false Seer, even going so far as to stretch out his hand to help her.

"You bastard! That's mine! She stole that from me; she doesn't deserve it!" Meshi's temper snapped under the weight of this fresh betrayal.

Meshi dragged out the stake he'd snagged during their scuffle with the squire and shoved Eria to the side. The cable threaded through the beast's mouth shifted as one of its holders went out of balance. Meshi pushed himself between the others and aimed the stake at Lees.

He clenched his fist and forced all of his rage into the handle. The dangerously coiled Hyper exploded from the stake and covered the distance in an instant to pierce Lees' outstretched hand.

The moment she opened the door leading out of Teeg's workshop, a bomb exploded in her hand. Piercing pain ignited across her nervous system, shutting off all sight and sound for an instant. She could sense bands of raw skin on her arms and legs, and something was holding her upright. But it was like Lees was half asleep and fighting to wake up, thrashing in deep water without a clear sense of direction.

Something was very, very wrong. Lees forced herself forward even though she was blinded, letting her injured hand fall to her side. Cramps seized her insides once more. She couldn't go back into the workshop. She had to keep moving. There was something there, something dangerous, and she needed to fight against whatever it was.

The miniature Hyper ball appeared by her side. Lees could sense it despite her lack of sight, and she mentally nodded to it. She couldn't fight without its help, isn't that what Ike had said?

Lees and the motionless beast screamed in unison. The gut-wrenching polyphonic screech sank into Meshi's bones and froze him in place. Teeg, Jez, the Enforcer, and a limp squire tumbled from the beast's jaws as it convulsed. Lees crumpled to the ground, and the beast's form splintered outward and shattered.

Teeg and Jez regained their feet quickly thanks to Ike. The Enforcer stayed prone, panting and grimacing from the wound that was seeping blood again. Meshi stared at Lees in horror. Her back arched as she arranged her knees beneath her.

Then her head snapped up to meet his gaze, face flat but eyes a burning blood red.

To Lees, it seemed that she was surrounded by shadowy figures lurking in the peripheries. The air was thick with smoke wherever she was, but she could see nothing beyond the immediate threat. The coil of Hyper in her hand snapped out and hovered in place next to her face as the wound in her hand healed rapidly. Shards of Hyper from the fallen beast carved pathways in the cobblestones as they stood on end and snapped together like puzzle pieces. Stalagmites of pure

Hyper formed behind Lees, then continued in a circular pattern until she and Meshi were boxed in together.

"Lees, no! Don't do this!" Teeg said.

Lees jumped to her feet from her knees and held out a hand.

"Want to see a new trick I learned?" She asked. Two voices were in her throat, speaking simultaneously at different pitches. The effect made the hair on Meshi's neck stand on end.

Lees held out her hand, palm facing Meshi. The tips of three stalagmites right behind Meshi snapped off and soared through the air, narrowly grazing the sides of his face on their path to Lees' hand, where they formed a wickedly sharp, straight-bladed sword that fit her grip perfectly. Meshi backed up automatically, but his path was blocked by stalagmites that stung his skin when they touched him.

"P-please, Lees, don't hurt me – you wouldn't – please," Meshi babbled.

Lees smiled cruelly and twisted her wrist so the blade danced through the air, making lazy figure-eights in the space between her and Meshi. The voices of those outside the Hyper circle faded as her vision narrowed on the boy who had caused her so much pain.

She stepped forward, blade aloft, savoring the look of terror on the little asshole's face.

Something bumped against her back and pressed her arms to her sides. Lees growled with two voices and struggled against whatever was holding her until the smell of peppermint and sawdust enveloped her.

"This isn't you, Lees. You're not like this. It's the stone, not you. You're a good person. Don't do this, you'll regret it. That Hyper Object – let her go, I want my daughter back, not this."

Teeg's voice was strained, like he was holding something back. Lees couldn't see how the Hyper stalagmites had sliced open his legs and stabbed into his sides, reopening the wounds that had already been closed twice now. Lees couldn't see the blood staining his clothes. She could only hear and smell and feel *home*.

"Come on, Lees, let the boy go. He's not worth it."

Let the boy go.

You're a good person.

I want my daughter back.

The scene around Lees illuminated. Shadow shapes with their blurred edges sharpened, familiar faces slowly coming into view. Her vision clouded over, trying to wrestle control away from her, but it wasn't strong enough to blind her anymore. Miniature Hyper vibrated inches from her face, sending her mental flashes like strobing warning lights. Lees released the sword and lifted her hand to the floating Hyper ball. Reluctance nibbled at the back of her mind, but Teeg's words held greater weight.

Wrenching herself from the depths of an ice-covered lake within her, Lees shed the last of her red Hyper coating and gave a strangled sob, collapsing into Teeg. The protective ring of stalagmites collapsed.

She tried to breathe in, but something was blocking her windpipe. Lees choked, sputtering and clawing at her face. In her desperation, Lees' nails dug into her lips and cheeks, leaving bloody trails in their wake. Teeg, bewildered and terrified, tried to pry her hands away until Lees finally pushed him off and rolled onto the ground face-first.

Jez, Ike, and the rest of the townspeople surrounded her – everyone except Meshi, who half-crawled to where the Enforcer sat hunched over himself. Teeg threw himself down next to Lees, grabbing at her wrists, shouting, "Lees! What's wrong? Stop! You're hurting yourself – what's happening?"

Lees stretched three fingers into her mouth. Her eyes bulged. Her lips were turning pale blue. She dug around, gagging and gasping, until a glistening red mass emerged. Tiny protrusions grasped her teeth, tongue, lips, anything they could grab, resisting her with all their might. Teeg, finally understanding, used his strength as leverage to draw her forearm back. Stretching its miniature tendrils to their breaking point, the object held fast to Lees' face for one long, agonizing moment.

Then, with a wet squelch, the painfully extracted Hyper slapped onto the ground. The collapsed stalagmite barrier shattered completely and bounded into the circle where Lees was hunched over, fusing with the Hyper she'd coughed out until the entire mass compressed back into the small, multi-faceted shape of the Hyper Object as if nothing had happened. Lees pulled air into her lungs messily, hyperventilating until color returned to her face.

"You did good kid." Teeg smiled at Lees. He put his hand gently on her face, then collapsed on the ground next to her. Jez and Eria were already pressing against his wounds to staunch the bleeding, and Ekoli ran off to locate the doctor.

"Hey! Tie those shitheads to a pole or somethin', would ya?" Jez snapped at the people closest to the Enforcer, Meshi, and the still-unconscious squire. They hastily got to work pulling rope from where they'd held down the beast.

"Hey – tell her it's not her fault, will ya? None of this, she didn't mean-you'll tell her, right?" Teeg asked Jez, his voice so hoarse and low she had to lean in to catch the words.

"That's one you're gonna have to handle, bud. You're not putting that conversation on me." Jez peeked under her hands at the wound on his side and applied more pressure. Teeg groaned, his eyebrows drawing together the harder she pressed.

"Promise you'll keep her company. I don't want her to be alone, after all this."

"Would ya shut up already? Jeez, you really piss me off when you talk like that," Jez replied.

Lees hovered on the line between awake and asleep. Teeg and Jez's voices floated in and out, but the words they said didn't make sense. She was aware of her hand moving, but she had no idea why until it grasped the Hyper Object. Lees tensed, but its visions were muted, less combative. Teeg's gruff face and patchy beard smiled warmly. With all that had happened, she couldn't quite tell if it was real or not.

Jez's voice came again, soft and gentle, but Lees' ears were too filled with static to parse it. She opened her eyes to see that beautiful woman patting her shoulder before hauling Teeg to his feet. Lees allowed Jeri, of all people, to help her stand and support her weight, as Jez was doing for Teeg. Her foot bumped something, and she carefully stepped over a piece of the Enforcer's broken hammer. The snarling lion looked much less threatening without its other half.

CHAPTER 18

Farewell Last Light

The hours following the Hyper beast's rampage flew by as the citizens of Last Light attempted to restore order. Ike spent a good chunk of that time bargaining with the burly miners over how they were handling the new captives.

"That squire's lookin' pretty rough too. Don't you think – *Meshi, shut up! You want to get slugged again?* – shouldn't she go see the doc too?" Ike asked Eria. Meshi muttered a fresh slew of insults at the mining crew, but kept himself safe behind Ike. Eria stared back but made no move to direct his crew.

"Come now, Eria, don't be like that. We're not barbarians. Untie those two and bring her up to the clinic. She'll need a bed," Dr. Hayes directed, returning to the square after tending to Teeg. He patted Eria on the shoulder and smiled warmly. "When you get there, tell Teeg he can head on home. He'll be fine now so long as he rests. A tall order, I know."

Eria nodded to his crew to follow the doctor's orders. Dr. Hayes adjusted his glasses to check Ike's arm. He gingerly held his wrist and turned the arm slowly, poking along the bone. "Seems to be healing just fine. You're an impressive fighter, Ike."

"Hey - get your hands off him. Stop talking to us like we're on your level," Meshi snapped. Ike pinched the bridge of his nose and squeezed his eyes shut. Dr. Hayes ignored Meshi's comment and reached out to inspect Meshi's ragged hands.

"That looks nasty, son. You better let me —"

"Don't touch me!" Meshi yanked his hands away, failing to hide the wince of pain when the scabs broke open across his palms again. "Come over here, Ike, away from *him* and the rest of them."

Dr. Hayes shrugged. He nodded to Ike before striding away after the crew members who were half-carrying the nearly-digested squire back to the clinic.

"You gotta work on those manners, Meshi."

"Shut up," Meshi said. He craned his neck to see if anyone was listening, then lowered his voice, "We need to retreat and regroup. Clearly, more firepower is needed to take down this backwards town. We can talk about your... disappointing actions today on the train ride home. Come on."

Meshi finally looked at Ike. He raised an eyebrow expectantly when Ike didn't move.

"What if we stayed? Help them rebuild a bit? A lot of this mess is our fault," Ike said slowly.

"Stay here? What, did you hit your head or something? Even the idea of staying makes my skin crawl. I want nothing more than to leave, take a hot bath, and scrub off the filth of these past few days." Meshi shivered. He cocked his head to where his bag was sitting at the top of the partially destroyed stairway to the train platform. "Get my things, then go figure out how we can leave. Pay someone off if you have to. The Enforcer can find his own way home. Don't imagine he'll hold that title for long after we explain to the Oppri how badly he failed."

"Meshi, you're not listening to me. I can't go with you."

Meshi snorted. "Of course you can. You don't owe these earthworms anything –"

"Except I do," Ike interrupted. He took a deep breath. Meshi stared at him in disbelief. "We both do. I'm not leaving here until we see that through."

"Must I remind you that you're under contract?"

"Forget the contract. Leaving right now, it's not right. You don't have to choose that path, Meshi. You could stay with me, we could help Lees together."

"I'm willing to move past you abandoning me when I needed your help and working against me to secure the Hyper Object from that girl. As far as I'm concerned, that's all in the past. But if you don't come with me, if-if you decide to stay – and you leave me – after everything we've been through?" Meshi's voice cracked. Two of the townspeople nearby didn't even bother trying to hide their eavesdropping. Meshi's cheeks burned pink. He cleared his throat too loudly and said haughtily, "Ike, this is your last chance to regain my favor."

As Ike stared at Meshi, an ice-cold fist gripped his heart. He took in the boy's grimy blond hair plastered across his forehead, his emerald-gray houndstooth vest coated in dirt and blood, and his filthy trousers. Meshi's bloodshot eyes were ringed with red. And those raw, lacerated hands.

"LET ME GO! I must see her!" The Enforcer bellowed. "She spared me, she let me live. My life is owed to her – the Hyper Object showed mercy, I don't understand!"

With only half his armor still intact and down to one arm, the townspeople were far less intimidated by the Enforcer now. He struggled against his bindings in vain, kicking and flailing in the direction of anyone who got too close.

The people standing guard backed away with their hands up.

"Lees musta knocked this guy silly, he's talkin' nonsense."

"He's mad that he's not dead? Jeez, nothing'll satisfy these guys, huh?"

Eria huffed and pointed at his crew. "That's it! Train's leaving right now. Garrey, go find the engineer and drag him here if you gotta. I've had enough of this nonsense. The rest of you, get that shiny asshole on board." He rounded on Ike and poked a finger into his chest. "That kid's gotta get the hell out of here, too. You with him or you stickin' around?"

"Give me a minute," Ike growled. Eria tapped his wrist dramatically. Ike pressed Meshi's shoulder to push him closer to the train station. "Listen, Meshi, now's our chance. We can start over. We can help Last Light rebuild. With your family's influence, I'm sure —"

Meshi gasped. He spat in Ike's shocked face and stepped toward the platform, shooting his former bodyguard and companion a disappointed look before hissing, "You dare bring my family into this? As if they'd help a traitor." Meshi thrust his chin away from Ike and seethed. Then, a slow smirk crossed his face. "Hmm. This is all for Anise, isn't it? Trying to wriggle your way into their good graces? Hah! You really are a fool, Ike. That woman never loved you. How could she? You're just a —"

Ike's vision went red. He wrapped his hands around Meshi's collar and shoved him against the side of the train car. Meshi yelped in surprise. Ike shoved his forearm into Meshi's sternum, leaving his other hand free to reach to his side.

Meshi chuckled darkly. "There he is! There's the Ike I know. A brute through and through."

"All right, that's enough!" Eria snatched up Meshi's bag and stomped over to where Ike still had Meshi pressed against the train. Garrey returned to the platform with a uniformed man in tow, who anxiously scuttled into the locomotive cabin while avoiding eye contact with the raving Enforcer. Ike's fist holding Meshi's collar tightened as Eria's crew surrounded them, each trying to pry them loose and push the boy closer to the train.

Pressure grew from the crowd. They pushed and pulled until finally managing to wrench the boy free from Ike's iron grip. Meshi tripped on the stairs, caught in the many hands pressing him forward. Eria threw the duffel bag through the train's open doors.

"You're really going to let me leave alone?" Meshi asked quietly.

Ike looked around at Last Light – or at least, what was still standing. They'd barely been here for two days, and it would take months, maybe years, for them to rebuild what they'd done.

Ike opened his mouth, but the words died on his tongue. He unclenched his fists, the lines on his face smoothing, and stepped aside to allow Eria to take over. The disgruntled miner rushed forward to practically drag Meshi through the train doors. Meshi's face suddenly contorted, wild rage overpowering reason.

"Mark my words, Ike. I'll hunt Lees down and watch her bleed out! Then I'm coming for you! There's nowhere you can hide! I swear it!"

Eria tapped the window next to the engineer, who jumped at the noise so violently he hit his head against the ceiling.

The doors slid shut, muffling Meshi's ranting that continued until the train was out of view. Ike simply stared at the tracks blankly.

No matter how hard he tried, Ike couldn't remember how long they'd been together. A year? Two? More? It certainly felt like they'd known each other for a lifetime. Memories surfaced and faded. Meshi, composed and sheltered, finally explaining the origin of his pendant after weeks on the road. But where was that boy? Meshi's bright-red face swam into view, spit flying as he cursed Ike's name and family at the top of his lungs.

The contract, the money, his employment. Foolish pursuit of the Hyper Object. What did any of that matter when it turned a sweet, underachieving boy into... *that?*

"Never really know someone until they're backed into a corner," Eria commented. Ike nodded absently, still watching the now-vacant tracks in a daze, Meshi's words fresh in his head.

Lees stared at the familiar ceiling of her room above Teeg's workshop, tracing the latticework of exposed beams overhead with her eyes. The Hyper Object radiated gentle heat from where it sat on her bedside table. Exhaustion threaded itself through every muscle in her body, though any pain had been reduced to a dull ache. Her open wounds had stitched themselves back together over the course of the last few hours without Dr. Hayes' intervention.

She'd been told to stay put, so she was. Random bits of the day's events popped in and out of her thoughts like puzzle pieces refusing to form the full picture. She flipped through a mental catalog of the worst emotions she'd felt – pain, terror, longing, bitterness – but what were they attached to? How much of it was her, and how much of it was the object's?

Jingling keys accompanied heavy footsteps up the stairs. Nobody in the world carried as many keys as Teeg. The front door swung open too fast and smacked the wall behind it. *Every time*, Lees thought with a smile. Teeg's heavy boots stomped through the narrow hallway and into the living room. Jez greeted him, but her words were too muffled for Lees to understand. Teeg grunted something in reply.

Two sets of footsteps moved into the kitchen as the conversation continued. The words were lost as they drifted through the wall to Lees' room until all she could make out were their tones. Deep, rumbling Teeg and smooth, syrupy Jez. After a few minutes, a tea kettle whistled shrilly, followed by the gentle tinkling of glasses being pulled from the cabinet by the sink. *Lopsided green clay mug, Hyper-embossed Eye of Mite mug with a chip around the rim, the thick, pewter mug with the awkward handle*, Lees predicted, though of course she couldn't pick out the individual cups in their collection from sound alone.

Lees closed her eyes to focus on the sounds, picking out

Teeg's heavy, slightly irregular footsteps from Jez's quick movements. He padded around the kitchen and into the hall, and Lees strained her ears to track his path, willing him to head towards her.

His footsteps paused on the landing, and the silence stretched on, broken only by the old fan buzzing in front of the window, doing its best to push air from one side of her room to the other.

Lees' sore muscles protested when she sat up. She paused, feet dangling over the side of her bed, but the house and workshop were still silent. Her bare feet hit the ground, and she slowly walked to the door, not bothering to put her boots on before reaching for the door. Lees pulled it open to reveal a very surprised Teeg. He stood right at her door, carrying a steaming green clay mug and another chipped black mug, then barked out a laugh.

"Knew you weren't asleep. Get back in that bed," Teeg urged. He followed her over and sat at the edge of her bed. Lees hugged her knees and assessed his injuries, taking in his bandaged hands, swollen nose, and the expertly sewn stitches holding his cuts together.

Lees noticed Teeg doing the same thing to her, and she cracked a smile. He set the green mug on her bedside table, giving the Hyper Object a wide berth.

"That thing don't look like much besides a rock now," Teeg noted. He cleared his throat and lowered his voice to say, "I can't tell you how scared I was seein' you like that."

Whatever it was about the combination of those words, the look on Teeg's face, and the days of sustained panic released the pressure building in Lees' chest. Tears welled in her eyes as the floodwaters broke, and between sobs that shook her body, Lees explained everything.

Visions of her childhood home and mother, Teeg's grave and then her own, grotesque scenes of violence, pain, suffering – the miniature Hyper Object inside the imaginary workshop, the desperation to stop the Enforcer from destroying Last Light, the fear of the orb they'd found deep within the mines. Learning how to shape Hyper, losing control of her mind and body. Meshi trying to kill her, the Enforcer trying to kill her, everybody trying to kill her.

Teeg listened patiently, at times reaching for her but stopping before he made contact. By the time Lees's ramblings ended, the tea beside her was stone cold.

"It-it was you. Your voice. And Jez's. I heard you, but like I was underground miles away. You pulled me out, both of you. I-I'm so sorry Teeg, your wife's coat –" Lees said.

"Uh-uh, stop right there. I won't have you apologizin' for defending yourself. All I care about is that you're safe and that *thing's* out of you." Teeg shifted on the bed and took a sip of tea, grimacing at the cold liquid. He stared down at his mug and, without looking up, said slowly, "Look, I don't get this object thing. What it is, or what it can do. And I don't know what being a *Seer* means for you. It... this whole thing scares me. But you're still you, ya know? You're a good person, and you'll do the right thing. I'm... well, I'm proud of you, kid."

Lees rested her chin on her knees, painfully aware of the seconds ticking by, until she finally managed, "Thanks, Teeg. I... thanks."

Teeg cleared his throat loudly and slapped his knee. "Now I gotta get back out there. Lots of work to be done. You, uh, hungry at all? No? Well, doc says you need rest, so you better not leave this bed, got it?"

Lees grabbed Teeg's hand. There was still blood on his collar, his face was still swollen, he was in bad shape – *he* needed rest, to be taken care of, but he was going back out to do what was right himself instead. She bit back the urge to beg him to stay.

"Teeg, I... I didn't have the best father growing up –"

"I know," Teeg interrupted. He patted her hand and smiled, "You didn't. But you know what? I got the best daughter." He pulled her into a crushing hug that made her bones hurt, but she clung to him and returned the embrace as best as she could. Teeg kissed her forehead and squeezed one more before letting her go.

Teeg crossed the room and paused at the door. "This is your room, kid, and this is your home. Always has been, always will be."

Those heavy, familiar footsteps moved slowly down the stairs, and the handrail creaked from his full weight. He moved slowly into the workshop, gathered a bag of tools, and then headed out into the street.

The sulphuric smell of burning coal drifted into the room. Lees picked up the Hyper Object and rolled it between her fingers. That something so small could cause such tragedy was amazing. Terrifying and cruel, but awesome nonetheless. Light from the hallway illuminated a strip of her room through the cracked door. The Hyper Object glittered in the light, casting crimson dots across her duvet and the wall.

Meshi would be back. He'd return with more knights of the Holy Cutlass Order, people even stronger than the Enforcer. It could be a while, but they'd eventually return. Would Last Light survive another attack? Would Teeg? Would *she*?

Lees dropped the Hyper Object onto the bed. It had been suspiciously quiet since she'd returned to the house, but there was no need to provoke it into causing another cascade of distressing visions.

If the object were gone, maybe they'd leave Last Light alone. If she could send it away somehow, force it out of the town—

The Hyper Object rolled on its own across the duvet until it bumped into her splayed fingers.

"You'd follow me back, wouldn't you?" Lees said flatly.

There really was only one way to keep her family and home safe.

Lees pocketed the Hyper Object and stood up again. She

paused, listening for Teeg's returning footsteps or Jez's quiet movements, but the house was quiet once more. They must have left together, satisfied she was safe and sound in bed.

She quickly pulled out her navy canvas bag and began to pack. Lees threw in an armful of hand-me-down clothes and carefully tucked her green knitted socks on top. She gulped down the bitter, ice-cold tea to empty the mug, then wrapped it in a sweater – Teeg wouldn't mind. This was the one she always drank out of anyway. Lees turned, and her heart sank as she stared at the wall of shelves Teeg had helped her install. They were a necessity to support her... *habit*.

Every inch of her shelves was lined with found treasures. Colorful Hyper-less rocks she'd found below ground. Pocket watches, charcoal pencils, and other trinkets left behind at Jez's bar by patrons too drunk to remember to retrieve them. Mechanical creatures made of cogs and welded metal scraps from Teeg's workshop. Wrenches, a soldering iron with a broken tip, and drill bits of every size. Half-filled notebooks, an Oppri holiday cookbook, and an instruction manual for repairing industrial mining drills.

Lees looked at her half-full bag and back to the shelves, then sighed. Feeling proud of her restraint, she opted only to bring the least used notebook, a metal possum wearing a top hat that raised it when wound correctly, and one pocket watch with an embossed logo of twin swords crossed in front of an open book. She didn't recognize the logo, nobody did, but it still told time decently accurately.

I won't be gone forever, Lees assured herself. *I'm going to deal with this thing and then come home. I'm going to fix this before anybody else comes to mess with Last Light.*

She tried not to think about Teeg's reaction when he realized she was gone – or Jez's when Lees didn't come to find her. *I won't write a note. I won't be away for that long. They'll understand, even if they're mad for a while.*

Slinging the bag over her shoulder, Lees surveyed her room one more time before stepping into her boots and pushing the window fully open.

This window was handy for repairs on the Rapidite glowing sign directing people to the workshop. Every so often, the cracked plate of yellow Hyper began to vibrate against the frame, which meant Teeg had to squeeze himself over the windowsill to the flat rooftop section to wrestle its housing back into submission.

Lees quietly lowered the window, picked up her bag, turned, and barely stopped herself from toppling over the roof.

Jez took a long drag of her cigarette before saying, "Where're you off to?"

You could technically reach the overhang from the living room on the first floor, but it required you to do a full weight pull-up to reach it. Lees could see now that the window was wide open. Jez sat with her back to the building's siding, holding a mug of what looked suspiciously like vinium.

"Uh, just, you know, fresh air. Good for the head juices,"

Lees babbled, her brain scrambling to catch up. "Air to clear my head, and it's a good view of the town – and wait, hang on. Why are you here? Right outside my window?"

"Like you said, good view out here." Jez took another drag. The plume of spiced smoke fogged the yellow light from the sign. "Lees, I know that it's been a long day, and you –"

"Stop. I'm sorry," Lees rushed to say. If Jez was about to make a big speech, or chew her out for what she'd done, or whatever – this wasn't the time for it. Jez's eyebrows shot up, stunned. "I have to leave. I don't know what else to do right now. The stone is attached to me, and-and I think I'm attached to it, so I can't just throw it away somewhere. And-and if we stay – me and the object – then everybody is in danger. They'll keep coming back and hurting people, I-I mean, they set the mine on fire!" Lees' ears burned – she could hear her voice rising and warbling as the words jumbled around. "I have to go fix this, however I do that, so I can come back. So everything can go back to normal!" Lees petered out, heart pounding in her ears. She tried to rein in her breathing.

Jez exhaled once more and stubbed out her cigarette. She stood up and stretched. "Yeah, I get it. Okay," she said. "Let me grab my bag from the bar, and we'll head out."

Lees blinked in rapid succession. Jez eased herself over the edge of the rooftop and stared back. "You need a hand gettin' down or?"

"Wait, no, no, you can't come with me. That's the whole

point I was trying to make. If you come with me, you'll be a target too. I-I won't put you in danger like that," Lees stuttered.

Jez rolled her eyes. "Wasn't askin', babe. Come on," She drained the mug of vinium and set it on the living room windowsill, then lowered herself from the rooftop by her fingertips. She gracefully dropped down to the street below. Craning her neck to see Lees still rooted to the spot, Jez propped her hands on her hips and growled, "I said, *come on!*"

"You about done?" Jez asked. They reached the street where the Eye of Mite sat after encountering almost nobody along the way. Much of the smaller debris and garbage had already been cleared, but it was clear it would take more than a few days to return the town to normal.

"Not until I convince you to stay! You saw what the Enforcer was like. What if he targets you? And Meshi, he's nuts, he could do anything," Lees argued.

"That kid doesn't scare me, and the Enforcer's down an arm. Think I'll manage."

"You're not listening to me!"

"Lees, when you say shit like that, you sound like a child. I *am* listening to you." Jez placed her hands on either side of Lees' face to cradle her cheeks. Her fingers gently threaded through Lees' hair. "Now *you* need to listen to *me*. Nothing you say is going to change my mind. I'm not letting you leave this town alone." Lees' scrunched-up face relaxed. She nodded, savoring the feeling of Jez's warm hands.

Jez gave Lees a lopsided smile and continued walking, calling over her shoulder, "You wouldn't last a minute out there without me anyway."

They reached the intersection next to the Eye of Mite, now much darker with only one unbroken streetlight, and stopped. Ike was pacing beside the front door. He noticed them after a lap and waved awkwardly. "Evening, ladies."

"Oh, gods," Jez groaned.

"I'm, uh, don't mean to startle you..." Ike rubbed the back of his neck. He swallowed hard, then started over, "I don't work for Meshi anymore. He's, I don't know, he's changed. I know you didn't mean for this to happen, but now that the Hyper Object has been found, the whole empire will be after you."

"Because of you. You and that little asshole. All of this is your fault," Jez snapped.

"I know you're mad. You have every right to be. But if you can trust me –"

"Trust you? The cutlass who came here ready to tear apart the town for a stone? Who called in backup that almost killed Teeg, and Lees, and me!?" Jez snorted and made to walk into the Eye of Mite, but Lees stopped her.

"We should at least hear him out," She said.

Ike looked grateful and nodded. "I have the same information as Meshi about how the Hyper Object works. I can teach you its history, the lore, all of it. And I'm not too bad in a fight." Jez snorted again and rolled her eyes. Ike ignored her and directed his next comment at Lees, "You're leaving town, right? I can help you use that object without getting hurt."

"What, be our travel buddy? Come along on an adventure? Give me a break. Absolutely –"

Lees pushed forward, cutting off Jez and putting herself between them. "Why are you doing this, Ike? Really. I want the truth." Jez mimicked Lees' narrowed gaze and joined her in staring the man down.

Ike picked at a seam on his shirt sleeve, then thrust his hands into his pockets and rocked back on his heels. Finally, he sighed and said, "There's someone I need to get back to. If she knew I turned my back on someone who needed help, especially if it's from a mess I caused, well, I wouldn't be able to face her." Jez threw her hands up in the air, but Lees stepped forward.

"All right," She said. "Yes. You can come with us." Jez sputtered in reply. Lees spun around to face her. "I know you don't trust him. But I don't want this thing to hurt you ever again. If he can help me with that... then you'll just have to get used to him being around."

Jez chewed her lip, then abruptly smacked Ike's chest. "If you so much as think about turning us in or hurting Lees, I will put you in the ground." She composed herself and gestured to the door. "Shall we?"

Lees fought back a smile and she followed her in.

The Eye of Mite exploded into cheers and whistles the moment Lees stepped through the door. People were standing shoulder-to-shoulder in the tiny bar, and the noise level rose even higher when the door closed behind Lees, Jez, and Ike.

"She rallies!"

"Lees, you're a beast!"

"Dunno how, but you sure showed those Oppri bastards!"

Lees grabbed Jez's shirt and pulled her down to eye level. "This isn't quite the discrete goodbye I was imagining. Did you do – whoa!"

Woodrow, Ekoli, and Garrey ripped Lees from Jez and shoved drinks in her hand. At their urging, Lees tipped back the shot glass and coughed. Another replaced the empty one immediately. Beer sloshed onto her boots as the rowdy group fought to reach Lees to congratulate her.

Jez slipped away behind the bar. Ike stood in the doorway, frozen in place, eyes scanning for anyone who might have their sights set on evening a score. One of the miners from the square approached him and held out a foaming glass.

"Saw what you did back there. Might not approve of your choice of friends, but anyone willing to risk their neck for us is part of the crew," The man said. Ike tentatively reached for the beer, and the man clinked glasses enthusiastically. Ike grinned and downed the glass in one gulp, nearly spitting it right back up when Eria excitedly slapped him on the back.

Jez opened the register and pulled half the bills out, pocketing the cash before thrusting one, two, three full bottles into her own duffel bag.

"Oh my gosh, help!" Lees squealed, resurfacing from the crowd and slamming into the bar. She reached for Jez, but Ekoli was already pulling her back.

Laughing, Jez turned and found herself face-to-face with an annoyed Midge.

"So, what, you're leaving?" Midge asked. She filled three pints at once and slid them across the bar. They were snatched up immediately and replaced by six empty glasses.

"It's gotta be done," Jez replied. Eylii popped in from the back with a plate of freshly fried shaved roots. She handed it off to an impatient patron and immediately got to work washing dishes. "I'll miss you fools."

Eylii dropped the soapy glass and spun around. Tears were already welling in her eyes as she threw her arms around Jez. "Leaving!? No! You can't go!"

"Okay, okay, thanks for the concern," Jez said, peeling the younger woman off her. "You'll be fine, and I'll be back."

"You can't just walk out of here. This is your bar! People need you! What's the point of all that fighting if you're just going to leave?" Midge complained. She shooed Jez away from the ice machine and filled a row of glasses. Then she scooted Jez over so she could reach the bottles behind the bar to make the drinks.

"Seriously, pull me over the bar, this place is cra-*aaaah*!" Lees resurfaced and then vanished again, her words already slurred.

"Be right there!" Jez called through her laughter. "Midge, I gotta help her. It's not her fault what happened, and it's not safe to stay."

"You're just abandoning us then?" Midge snapped. She handed over the herb-seltzer drinks and started filling three pitchers from the beer tap.

"Don't be so dramatic, Midge."

"You should talk! Running away with your girlfriend when there's all this work to do?"

"She needs me more than you all do. What d'you need me for, breaking up bar fights and hauling kegs? You'll be just fine without me for a while," Jez assured her. She pulled the zipper up on her bag harder than she meant. Lees pushed away an overflowing pitcher someone was trying to get her to drink from. Ike edged along the wall to reach behind the bar, trying and failing not to bump anyone along the way.

Jez grabbed Midge's wrist and slapped a set of keys into her palm. "Keep the lights on until I get back, would ya?"

"Wait, what? Me? I can't run the bar! I don't have your particular, uh, what is it Eylii says? Jenesaquaa?"

"I believe it's actually pronounced je ne sais quoi," Erish supplied, punctuating his point with a loud hiccup.

The bar door opened, and roughly half of the bar turned to watch Town Chief Marshall and three of his chippers attempt to slink in unnoticed. Silence fell over the bar.

"We don't want trouble. We thought maybe a burger, a couple drinks..." Town Chief Marshall muttered, taking off his hat and fidgeting with the brim.

Jez smiled. She hoisted the bag over her shoulder and patted Midge's back. "Don't look at me. It's Midge's bar now. What say you?"

Midge beamed, puffed out her chest, and shouted, "Get the fuck out of my bar! This is the Eye of Midge now, and we don't serve guard dogs for the Oppri."

Jeers and whoops of agreement followed the group back out into the street. Lees finally stumbled forward and dragged herself over the bar into the staff area. Jez pulled her to her feet and motioned for them to follow her into the kitchen.

Jeri's head poked out from the top of the hammock as the trio walked past.

Buoyed by the rapid succession of shots and beers, Lees squinted at him and slurred, "Enjoy your nap, you lazy asshole."

"Eat shit, Lees!" Jeri replied cheerfully. Jez hauled Lees forward and led both her and Ike to the back door. She turned to Jeri, who had hopped down to the ground. "I'm gonna miss her," He said wistfully.

Jeri reached over to hug Jez, lifting her off the ground

until she smacked his shoulder playfully. He put her down and looked at her bag on the ground.

"You gonna go see mom?" He asked.

"You don't gotta call her that, we don't live there anymore. And I hope not!"

"Well, if you do… send my regards."

"I can't take that woman in a fight! You'll have to do your own dirty work, Jer."

Jeri nodded. He climbed into his seat in the Burgermaker machine and cracked his knuckles. "You headin' east?"

"Yep," Jez said. She saluted him, picked up her bag, and followed after Lees and Ike.

Jeri entwined his fingers in the machine, and the Burgermaker came to life. He pulled a lever and plucked the Hyper strings wound deep within its machinery. The other appliances in the kitchen shifted away from the back left corner of the room, revealing a passageway descending into the ground.

"Tunnels again!?" Lees groaned.

"Get used to them!" Jez said. She switched on Lees' lantern and led the way. The three of them disappeared into the tunnel below. Jeri counted to ten, then shifted the machines back into place. He lit a cigarette and put a foot up on the console, staring absently at the countertops.

A tiny ding drew his attention to the serving window, where Midge was sliding a slip of paper with an order. "Look alive! Burger with the works."

Jeri groaned. He balanced the cigarette in his mouth and yanked the yellow Hyper to fire up the machine, pulling more gently than usual.

As the train clicked along the tracks through a long stretch of tunnel, the occupied carriage was silent. Nothing was visible beyond the windows save for the occasional flash of Rapidite lighting the way. The battered squire had fallen asleep almost immediately. The Enforcer's incoherent ranting had fallen to a quiet muttering.

Meshi sat alone, working up the courage to finally look at his hands. He slowly unbandaged the first one. Bruised puncture marks decorated his palm. Some of the lacerations cut so deeply that he was sure the tendons were ripped to shreds. Flattening his fingers was impossible. Using his teeth, he unwrapped the bandage on his other hand. He bit the inside of his cheek to stop himself from crying out. The painkillers were wearing off.

His duffel bag shifted on the seat next to him. Meshi watched in surprise as something wiggled in the front pockct. Gingerly, he unzipped it using the knuckles on two fingers. His pendant necklace tumbled out onto the seat beside him, the cracked orange stone glowing brightly.

"Where did you... I thought I lost you," Meshi mumbled. He craned his neck to see if either of his companions had noticed, but they hadn't moved. Slowly, he picked up the pendant and slid it over his neck. It yanked outward and hovered over his hands. He studied the orange stone, which was now pulsating urgently.

Bracing himself for the pain, he carefully pulled the stone from its gold housing. It expanded to loop around his fingers. Meshi watched in amazement as the edge of the deepest cut on his left palm pressed together, the wound stitching up before his eyes. The pain was gone – it burned, but the sensation was nothing compared to before. Other cuts were pulling themselves together, the purple and green bruises fading back to his normal skin tone.

Meshi watched the stone heal his wounds and smiled.

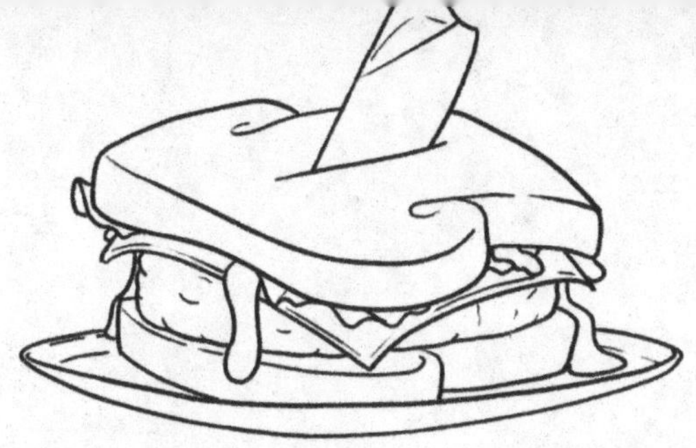

Vol. 2 Bonus Chapter

Found Family

Two months to the day after her unceremonious exile to Last Light, Lees drags herself to the Eye of Mite to nurse a drink alone and feel sorry for herself. Her brooding is interrupted when an attractive bartender catches her eye, but Lees barely has time to introduce herself before Teeg and the townsfolk try showing this new mite how to have a little fun. After a rambunctious evening, she helps Teeg stumble home. Absorbed with her own misfortunes as she is, Lees' journey to their shared house forces her to see this town – and her life – in a new light.

Read this bonus chapter for free at:

hyperobject.ink/found-family

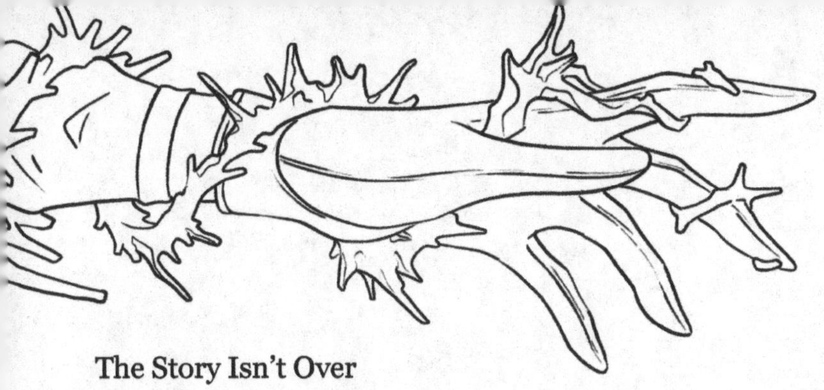

Your next adventure in the Keeperverse is coming soon.

If you're enjoying Hyper Object, here is a sneak preview from our upcoming book Keeper.

Hazel's world is disappearing. The phenomenon elimi-nating Traxia piece by piece is accelerating, and the Keepers are powerless to stop it. Frustrated by the Council's inaction,

Hazel disobeys orders to investigate herself – and ends up face-to-face with an enemy that hasn't been seen in decades. With the help of her reluctant companions, Hazel must find a way to recover her powers and save two worlds from destruction.

The Witch Hazel

High up in the mountains, the late morning sun illuminated a region that was perfectly still, save for one lone figure winding its way through the trees.

Hazel wasn't technically supposed to be out here alone. Standard expedition protocol along the northern mountain region called for Keepers to be accompanied by a minimum of two Traxian soldiers. Mt. Tuocs' peak rose high above the cloudline, and the sharp drop-offs and thin air created tricky situations for the careless.

Since this wasn't an official mission, she reasoned that this wasn't exactly breaking protocol. That hadn't stopped her from taking precautions by waking up before first bells and taking the longer, more cumbersome route here.

The fresh snow on the mountainside sparkled in the light of the rising sun, and Hazel delighted in crunching through the untouched snow blanketing the little forested valley between peaks. She moved briskly to stave off the cold. Every breath billowed out in white plumes around her face, and her cheeks burned despite the thick yellow cloak pulled tightly up over her face. Not even the trees growing in dense clusters this high up could slow the icy wind whipping through the valley.

Hazel was taller than most Keepers her age if you measured up to the tips of her triangular ears. Usually this worked in her favor, but traveling through the forest meant it slowed her down. She'd been constantly ducking low-slung branches and brushing away needle-line leaves caught in her fur all morning. Despite the distractions, Hazel carefully scrutinized each tree and plant for signs of disease or distress as she walked.

"Traxia?" Hazel called, craning her neck to survey the full height of a nearby tree. She traced one finger along the counterclockwise swirls in its bark. "Those amber cankers on the *ymrots pines* here, is that a fungus? Looks like it's spreading upward and drying out the branches."

<Yes, Hazel,> the Source Traxia responded.

Hazel unconsciously swiped at the fur on her right temple, a habit she'd formed as a child when a piece of the Source's power had first entered her body. When she became a Keeper and accepted the Source, Traxia's voice had hung uncomfortably between her ears like a deep itch she couldn't scratch. But that was years ago. She'd long since gotten used to the sensation.

"Tell me what's causing it."

Her vision clouded as the Source flashed a looping animation in her head. Tiny cartoon-like spores traveled up through the severed roots of a tree before spreading to other trees nearby.

<Root damage appears to be the culprit. The damage created an entry point for the fungal spores and weakened the tree's defenses,> Traxia continued.

"It'll spread if we leave it. Traxia, cull the infected limbs and draw out the spores – minimize further damage to the tree when you do and seal up any wounds. Oh, and bubble the spores," Hazel commanded. She crouched and held her hands near the tree's base. The familiar sensation of the Source stretched out from her fingers as it pulled the spores from beneath the bark. Though she couldn't see it, Hazel could feel the nearly invisible particles follow a reverse path from their entry points before they swirled before her. A perfect transparent bubble appeared around the spores. Hazel tucked the bubble into the pouch slung over her shoulder.

While this tree might survive today, others would suffer a similar fate. Not just on this mountainside, where Hazel had been attempting to heal the damage for weeks, but across the region and beyond. Unless they could figure out a way to stop what was severing underground root structures and sapping away water, minerals, and life, it was only a matter of time before the entire forest died.

Hazel continued forward, noting every bent branch and wilted plant on the forest floor. Something was whining nearby – a desperate, high-pitched sound that cut through the frigid stillness. She snapped to attention and rushed forward.

At the edge of a small clearing, tangled in the roots of a twisted tree, a horned goat was bleating and struggling to free its antlers. The animal was just a few feet in length with disproportionately large horns jutting out of its forehead. It seemed as though the rest of its body had not quite caught up with the growth. One of the horns was hooked around an exposed root and held the animal nearly pinned to the ground. A cluster of berry bushes grew tantalizingly close, as if a carefully laid trap.

"Traxia, how old is this little fella? Has his venom come in yet, or can I touch him?"

<This horned mountain goat appears to be approximately one year old. At this age, its venom would likely knock you unconscious for several hours. I would suggest you avoid being gored. With the low temperatures in this area, you would likely perish before – >

"Yeah, yeah, thanks, got it," Hazel interrupted.

She slowed her approach and tried to move as calmly as possible, taking care to steer clear of the venomous points of its antlers. The horned goat's eyes widened as Hazel closed the distance and it thrashed wildly.

"Hey, hey, it's ok. Sorry little guy, looks like you're in quite a mess," She whispered gently. "Will you let me help you out?"

Hazel sat back on her heels and rested both hands flat against the loose blue material of her pants. She stayed stock still for a moment, avoiding eye contact with the terrified creature, and looked for signs of pain or an injury. The creature stopped struggling and rolled its yellow eyes toward her, then let out a low whine. Hazel crawled forward and circled around to reach the bushes. She plucked a cluster from its depths and held it out toward the trapped creature.

The trapped goat hesitated, eyed Hazel suspiciously, then reached forward to devour the berries. Hazel seized the moment of distraction and grasped the trapped horn firmly at its base. The goat screeched and bucked again, but Hazel held on. Working as quickly as she could, Hazel pulled back the troublesome root and threaded the horn from its grasp.

"Traxia, put up a shield the moment I let go… just in case," Hazel murmured. She took a deep breath and let go, simultaneously propelling herself backward in the snow.

Now free, the horned goat thrashed once more. The vicious point of its venomous horn punctured the space where Hazel's face had just been before bouncing off what appeared to be an invisible barrier. It shook its head comically, then bleated once more before bounding off.

"You can drop the shield now," Hazel said.

<Understood. I am required to inform you that was an unnecessary risk,> Traxia stated.

"There's no way it would have freed itself. My job is to keep and protect. That's what I'm doing," Hazel scoffed.

Her knees were soaked from kneeling in the snow, and the tips of her fingers were losing feeling. She hopped up and down and rubbed her hands together before covering her ears. The velvety tips burned as she massaged warmth back into them. She looked up toward the tops of the trees swaying high above her in the freezing wind that was cutting through the thick material of her pants. Hazel bounced around like this for a moment, calculating whether it was worth it to expend the energy to summon an insulated shell or portable fire. *On one hand, warmer is nice,* she mused to herself. *But on the other, if I miscalculate and pass out, the last thing I need is to be rescued by –*

Hazel's thoughts were interrupted by an ear-splitting ringing sound emanating from within her own head.

<You requested an alert when we were within one hour of the ceremony. This is your alert. We should start our journey back to the city now,> Traxia said.

"Jeez, that was way too loud. Anyway, we've got time, I want to finish up here," Hazel said dismissively. Not wanting to give in by asking Traxia for heat, she rubbed her arms vigorously once more, then continued on.

The slightly-illicit journey's destination was just ahead. With every step, the ambient noises of the forest around her dimmed. No forest animal chittered from the trees or scurried through the undergrowth. A twinge of tension flared in her left shoulder and a familiar pit of unease gurgled in her stomach. Two more steps, and the tree line abruptly ended. Hazel now stood in complete, unnatural silence.

What lay ahead looked like the aftermath of some otherworldly disaster. A sharp, perfect line stretched nearly a quarter mile wide from this spot and extended hundreds of feet beyond – a perfect square of emptiness, as if the patch of land had been neatly cut out by some malevolent giant. Skeletons of severed trees decorated one side of this line, each one having been cleaved in half with almost surgical precision.

It had been thirty years since the phenomenon first happened. A brilliant light stretched down from the sky to outline an acre of grassland, the shape perfectly symmetrical. Within hours, the illuminated square of land vanished, leaving behind a burnt, desolate patch of nothingness. It was incomprehensible. There was no lightning, no fire, no sinkhole, no disaster to speak of. One moment it was there, and the next... it wasn't.

Then it happened again a year later, this time cleanly severing a rushing river stretching from one coast to the other. This one caused problems for the thousands of Traxians relying on the flow of fresh water, and emergency services were dispatched to help. It took the Keepers a month to carve and redirect the river.

The Traxian people had no end of colorful, dramatic names for this phenomenon: The Blight, the Desolation, Atia's Wrath, the Burning. But perhaps to tamp down panic, the Council preferred their soldiers, Keepers, and scholars to simply use *dead zones* in their reports.

Hazel stood at the threshold of this dead zone and prepared herself. She instructed the Source to pull a one-foot cube of undergrowth from the healthy side before stepping over the slice line, letting the cube of plantlife float in front of her.

"All right, you know the drill. Give me a full scan. Let's see if anything's changed," Hazel commanded.

The Source hummed in her head before a vision appeared in front of her eyes – a green grid stretched across the ground in front of her now with text scrolling along the bottom of her field of vision. Someone on the outside unfamiliar with Keepers would see Hazel standing stock still save for her tail, which flicked toward the right. But in Hazel's mind, Traxia was rapidly sharing updated information about the ground around her.

<*Calcium carbonate. Quartz fragments. Granite. Sand. Silicate,*> Traxia rattled off in a monotone voice. <*Nearly identical to the fourteen other analysis instances, Hazel. No organic material beyond what you introduced is detected.*>

"You're sure? Nothing? Not even nitrogen?"

<*Correct.*>

Hazel's stomach flipped. That assessment meant she knew even before approaching that the experiment was failing. Eight weeks ago, she'd begun planting a grid of 47 cubes identical to the one floating in front of her in the center of this dead zone. Once the Council had finished their assessment of the dead zone and vacated the area, she had snuck away to conduct her own tests. Whenever she could get away to visit, Hazel took cubes of healthy plant matter and planted them in the destroyed soil, taking care to meticulously water each one and measure its sun exposure. Up close now, only browning and wilting leaves stretched out weakly from the blackened dirt. With a nagging sense that all she was accomplishing was torturing and killing plants pulled from healthy soil, Hazel commanded the Source to dig out a square and bury the new cube.

A rain cloud formed above the little plot with a flick of Hazel's wrist, and she frowned as the water drizzled over the other plants in their various stages of death.

"So the fertilizer isn't working. We're not going to be able to reseed these dead zones, are we?"

What was going to happen when dead zones covered half the planet? Alumast and the other major cities were already overcrowded with displaced Traxians. Rivers had already been severed. Trade routes demolished. There was no rhyme or reason to where these swaths of wasteland appeared, which meant it was nearly impossible to predict where or when the beams of light appeared to signal the beginning of disaster. If they couldn't reseed, if they couldn't stop them from coming, how would they feed everybody? What would they do when habitats were destroyed? What —

A shrill siren sounded from just behind her forehead.

<*We are within a half-hour of the ceremony. If you want to attend, you must leave now,>* Traxia said.

"Gah - I need to change that alarm command. I'm almost done, then we can go," Hazel grumbled.

The rain cloud disappeared with a wave of her hand. She stared out at the withering plants and watched water droplets fall from their sagging stalks, trying not to feel hopeless. Though she'd set out before the sun rose this morning, it had taken nearly half the morning to reach this spot from the nearest teleporter. Hazel's tail twitched with impatience, a habit the Orator had scolded her for since childhood. There wasn't enough time to get everything done, especially not unsanctioned work. If she could just take a moment, just have space to think, she could figure out the next move...

"Maybe we're missing pollinators," She mused. But no living creature in the area would come close to the dead zone, even though it had been here for months. Bringing in the insects and other critters these plants relied on might help in the short-term, but what if those ended up dying, too? Hazel's chest tightened as an involuntary image of corpses littering the dead zone popped into her head – No, she couldn't risk that.

<Hazel, based on the command you issued this morning, we must leave now,> Traxia insisted loudly.

"FINE!" Hazel shouted. Her voice bounced around the empty space. "Let's fly to Alumast."

<Taking the teleporter might be faster, if you want to –>

"No, let's fly. Use the command set Flying Falcon Cloak."

Regardless of the Source's warnings or recommendations, Keepers were the ones in control. At her command, the Source flowed through her and extended beyond her own body. Behind her, Hazel's cloak parted with a satisfying snap. Debris on the forest floor – tiny pebbles and bits of minerals – rose and flew toward her to reinforce the fabric as it hardened into sharp curved wings spreading on either side of her. The front of her cloak wrapped around over and under her arms, securing the wings to her torso. She flexed her arms, making the faux wings shift and twitch with the movement.

<Ready when you are, Hazel,> Traxia said flatly.

Hazel jumped into the air with impressive speed and used her hands to manipulate the air around and below her to launch her skyward. Within seconds, the Source-aided breeze brought her hundreds of feet above her dead zone project. Frustration clouded her mind for a moment, but flying was the best way to clear her mind. She arched her wings and shot toward the ground, pulling up just above the snow-capped treeline. She looped once, twice, then jetted off toward the horizon in the direction of the city.

Acknowledgements

We want to thank all of our friends and family for their support and encouragement on this project. You've helped push us to create something beautiful not just for ourselves, but everyone that will read this.

We want to thank the many great storytellers that came before us, specifically Eiichiro Oda, Hiromu Arakawa, Michael Dante DiMartino, and Bryan Konietzko. We would not be the storytellers that we are without the inspiration of One Piece, Fullmetal Alchemist, and Avatar the Last Airbender. You set the stage, now we hope to stand up there with you.

I also want to thank my wife for all the support she's shown me through these years. Through the late night writing sessions, encouraging me every step of the way, offering me insights to the process, and celebrating every win we've had in creating this. She has truly been there for me when I've doubted myself the most.

– Mark

About the Authors

Shae Moloney lives in Minnesota and falsely believes the sub-zero-degree winters have made her a more resilient person. Shae's been telling stories her whole life, and when she's not writing professionally or recreationally, it's because she's being interrupted by her dog Lup. Her other published or recognized short fiction work includes *Practice Makes Perfect, The Neighborhood, On the Other Side,* and *Cowboys After Dinner.*

Kyle Keller has been staring at the inky black night sky and dreaming of fantastical worlds since he was old enough to have his first existential crisis. Since then, he hasn't stopped feverishly scrawling his stories onto any medium he could get his hands on from film, tv, books, comics, music, and digital. Kyle loves creating entertainment and bringing the characters in his mind to life in our world. Somehow he convinced Mark and Shae, two of the most talented people in the world, to be his lifelong creative partners and he is all the better for it. This book and all of his ideas would not exist without them.

Mark Sidener has worked in the film industry over the last 14 years, exploring many different creative projects in that medium. During that time, he co-founded Outer Giant Studios with his best friend Kyle Keller to take their creative spirits to the next level! Some would say over level 9000. As an avid lover of all things anime, Mark currently binges countless series with his beloved cat Ms. Peaches when he's not working on his own stories.

Thank you so much for reading

HYPER OBJECT

Volume 2

We'd like to extend a special thanks to:

Matt Owen
Dinah Kalaha
Nickie Henk
Sara Carolynn Kennedy
Kyla Finn
Lydia Sansom
Vik Govindarajan
Alex Bosch
Randi Nimz

And all of our Hyper Club supporters

For helping make this story a reality.

Thank you,
Kyle, Mark, & Shae

Back to work, ya Mite!

Follow Us

@outergiant

Read more Hyper Object at:

hyperobject.ink

Join our mailing list to receive alerts on our latest releases and deals.

outergiant.com

Go give this book to your friend!